WINNER - NEXT GENERATION BOOK AWARD
SHORTLIST - INDEPENDENT LITERARY AWARDS
FOUR "BEST BOOKS OF THE YEAR" LISTS

KERGAN EDWARDS-STOUT'S

SONGS FOR THE NEW DEPRESSION

"Kergan Edwards-Stout has crafted a work of fiction reminiscent of some classic tales in *Songs for the New Depression*. Even better, Edwards-Stout's debut boasts the kind of dark humor that made Augusten Burroughs (*Running with Scissors*) a household name." Advocate.com

"Simply stunning…" Dana Miller, Frontiers Magazine

"Compelling, beautifully written debut novel… The author's darkly comic, brutally honest prose reads like poetry and has a melodic flow that is equally funny and heartbreaking. Gabe's story is bittersweet, heartfelt and profound… A quintessential page-turner and the product of a truly gifted author." Edge on the Net

"From LA to Palm Springs to Paris, over the course of 20 years, Kergan Edwards-Stout takes us on a beautiful journey. The characters are dynamic, interesting, and real, and the relationships are painful and funny and romantic and sexy and sad all at once." Q Magazine

"Engaging debut. Edwards-Stout infuses reality and hopefulness into a bittersweet story about compassion and personal growth. A distinctively entertaining novel written with moxie and bolstered by pitch-perfect perspectives." Kirkus Reviews

"A thoughtful read that should appeal to many." Midwest Book Review

"The laughs make the book deceptively breezy. *Songs* shines with psychological truth and historical accuracy." A&U Magazine

"Brilliantly conceived and masterfully written… You'll read this once for its emotional impact and again to see how the author achieves it. But no matter how many times you dive in, you'll be impressed." Out in Print Reviews

"Edwards-Stout has written a wonderful book in which he takes on AIDS and depression from a personal point of view and he does so with great style and wit." Amos Lassen

"If a roller-coaster ride of sadness and humor sounds right up your alley, then look for *Songs for the New Depression*. This is the story of a man who knows he's dying, knows he's made a lot of mistakes in his life, and knows that he needs to fix things before the end. I won't tell you the end. Read the book." Terri Schlichenmeyer, *The Bookworm Sez* syndicated column

"This is a work that will make you both laugh and cry, and fair warning: it is difficult to get through certain portions of the text because Edwards-Stout is quite explicit in detail, which is testament to the fact that he is such a brilliant writer. This is not one to miss." Liberty Press

"*Songs for the New Depression* is an enjoyable and addictive read. In fact, don't be surprised if you find yourself not answering texts and neglecting your Facebook updates as you finish the book in one read. I did." Q Vegas Magazine

"Many tout this book as an important piece of fiction that should be read by all because of it's portrayal of AIDS. I'll give them that. I would add that it's not only an important piece of fiction because of the message, but it's a great piece of fiction writing regardless of the message." LGBT Book Review Blog

"The NY Times ought to be reviewing *Songs for the New Depression*, not the likes of me. It is a beautiful book, and, I think, an important one." Ulysses Grant Dietz, author of *Desmond* and *Vampire in Suburbia*

"Five Stars." Echo Magazine

"Kergan Edwards-Stout has written a masterpiece. A bravura debut novel, its heartfelt message is ultimately timeless. It is easily one of the top ten books I've enjoyed in the past decade. Once you start this one, you won't be able to stop." Carey Parrish, author of *Marengo* and *Big Business*

"Involving, emotional read... *Songs for the New Depression* touched me and stayed with me." Alfred Lives Here

"This is an incredibly important book." Chapters and Chats

"One of the most emotional, touching, heart-wrenching, and intelligent stories I've read in a very long time. With a dark wit reminding me of David Sedaris, this story examines the life of a man who's made many mistakes and, at the end, has managed to learn a few lessons... The language is sophisticated and elegant, each word precise, depicting clear images and evoking specific emotions. The description, whether of location, food, clothing, people, or emotions draws the reader into the moment as if it were actually happening. As a result, we experience Gabe's highs and lows on a powerful level, truly understanding Gabe, his limitations, and his dreams. Wrapped up in a sad story, illustrated with disappointments and heart-break, is a story of hope and understanding." Top2Bottom Reviews

"Kergan Edwards-Stout's *Songs for the New Depression* is a bold reminder that life, especially in its most difficult moments, is worth living. His characters are real and poignant, his writing is magical, and his message is timeless. Life is at its most precious when we are faced with our own mortality. It is an important book." Charles Perez, author of *Confessions of a Gay Anchorman*

"An affecting novel, written with great literary flair. I recommend it." Michael Nava, five-time Lambda Literary award-winning author, honored with the Bill Whitehead Lifetime Achievement Award for Gay and Lesbian Literature

DON'T MISS THE SNEAK PEEK OF
SONGS FOR THE NEW DEPRESSION
FOLLOWING GIFTS NOT YET GIVEN

GIFTS NOT YET GIVEN

AND OTHER TALES OF THE HOLIDAYS

Gifts Not Yet Given

And Other Tales of the Holidays

A Collection of stories by
Kergan Edwards-Stout

circumspect press

If you enjoy *Gifts Not Yet Given*, please leave a review on your favorite website, share with your friends, and spread a little holiday cheer—at any time of year!

Gifts Not Yet Given (and Other Tales of the Holidays)
Copyright © 2013 Kergan Edwards-Stout

C

circumspect press

Library of Congress Control Number: 2012918715
ISBN: 978-0-9839837-3-6 (pbk)
ISBN: 978-0-9839837-4-3 (ebk)
10 9 8 7 6 5 4 3 2 1

Book Jacket Design by Russell Noe
Author Photograph by Sara+Ryan Photography (http://saraplusryan.com)

Printed in the United States of America

To my family
Russ, Mason, and Marcus,
who expand my heart
each and every day of the year

Gifts Not Yet Given

And Other Tales of the Holidays

PREFACE

I TRIMMED THE FIRST OF OUR THREE TREES THIS WEEKEND. It is fake in terms of its material, but for me holds more emotional weight than any of our others. We also put up a real tree, which is cabin/rustic-themed, and a smaller tree in the boys' room, which holds their many handcrafted and super-hero ornaments. But it is the fake tree that always makes me cry.

Throughout the years, I have amassed an array of décor which serves as ornamentation; some Christmas-themed, some not. On every trip we take, I search, hoping to return with a unique found object which best captures the moment. The ornaments tell of specific times, places, and people, and the annual trimming usually leaves me in tears.

Some may ask, *why bother, if it hurts so much?*

There was a time in my life when I wouldn't allow myself to cry. I was afraid of what lay beneath my surface, certain that even the slightest crack in my veneer would provoke a flood the size of which it would be impossible to recover.

Eventually, however, I was faced with just such an emotional tsunami and found that I was somehow able to survive. Experiencing that flood enabled me to feel more fully and authentically alive. Survival is a badge of honor I proudly wear. I cherish each tear.

On the tree, there hangs a baby blue shoe to celebrate our eldest son's first year on earth. There is a handmade frame holding the first photo of our youngest, welcoming him into our home. There are also countless items collected together as a family: an angel made from cotton which came from Savannah, an art print from Paris, souvenirs from a journey to Italy, and remembrances from our recent vacation to Cape Cod. There are also toenail clippers from the Eiffel Tower and a bottle opener bearing a photo of the Pope, which came from my first trip to Europe with my partner Shane, who died in 1995.

And each and every one of our nutcrackers (currently 57 and counting) tells a story. Shane left his beloved collection to me, as his mother would give him German nutcrackers to commemorate special occasions. We've continued the tradition with our boys—they each get a nutcracker on Christmas Eve.

It is not the number of things we have, however, that is important. It is the stories they tell, the memories they encapsulate, and the emotions they trigger.

Many of the stories collected within this volume were originally given to loved ones as gifts themselves. They tell of the holidays, from Easter to Memorial Day, Fourth of July to Thanksgiving, and—of course—Christmas, offering a cornucopia of characters, themes, and tales which I hope will resonate, entertain, and maybe even conjure up a tear or two. Because if I'm sitting here crying as I trim my tree, then you can damn well cry too.

Tell your stories. Pass on your traditions. And feel every moment.

Kergan Edwards-Stout

THE
NUTCRACKER

THE NUTCRACKER

SHEILA WAS A BALL-BUSTER, no doubt. She knew it, and took a certain measure of pride in it. She'd earned the reputation, she reasoned, through her many years of study and continued career success. While playing nice might have made her more popular, would it have given her the corner suite? Likely not. There was no need for *warm-and-fuzzies* where work was concerned. Truth be told, even if she'd desired a different way to be, she knew no other. Growing up the daughter of Lou and Greta Mueller had left few options. Besides, knowing when to focus had served her well; she had seen no reason why she shouldn't continue in that mode. But the gift had thrown her.

Perhaps it was the way it was given, in the midst of the office holiday party, which angered her so. The entire company had gathered at the Minneapolis Airport Marriott to celebrate, and the Grand Ballroom had glowed with twinkling trees and garland. The faces of her co-workers glowed as well, lit from within by holiday spirits.

She'd felt off balance from the moment she entered the hotel lobby, regretting her decision not to invite Stanley. He would've come, if only for the free booze, but Sheila hadn't wanted to explain him. Not that anyone would've cared who he was, but lately he'd begun to feel like a weight around her neck, the proverbial albatross, and it made more sense to leave him at home. Walking toward the banquet room, however, it seemed everyone else was coupled, making Sheila feel even more alone.

But it was too late to turn back.

Catching herself in a hallway mirror, she glanced around quickly to make sure no one was watching before reaching up, her pinky deftly repairing a smudge to her bright red lipstick. The shade perfectly matched her gown. The Badgely Mischka had cost a small fortune, but Sheila felt that the impact it would have, further solidifying her reputation among her colleagues, would be well worth it. She loved her new haircut too, with its asymmetrical sides. She knew others would see it as severe, but Sheila savored her ability to surprise and dominate. Still, all the armor in the world couldn't stop her stomach from turning as she walked down the long corridor toward the Grand Ballroom.

Smile plastered in place, she soldiered on, as Lou and Greta had long taught, entering the room as if she owned it. Grabbing a glass of champagne off the tray of a passing waiter, she tried to nonchalantly chug it down, only to be cut off mid-sip by the appearance of pudgy Ryan from accounting. He'd poured himself into the same black suit he'd worn last year, with the reindeer light-up tie. Someone must have told him it was amusing, but to Sheila it just read as cheap. Due to drink or cold weather, his cheeks were even more red than normal. *It won't be too many years now,* Sheila thought, *until he can play Santa.*

Ryan approached, squeezing the hand of his equally porcine wife, Debbie. His hand held Debbie's so tightly, Sheila wondered if he meant to break it. Or if that showed just how much he dreaded interacting with Sheila.

"Ryan, *happy holidays!*" she cooed, as if they were dear friends.

"Sheila," he nodded in greeting. "You remember Debbie?"

"Of course!" Sheila exclaimed, pulling a surprised Debbie to her for a quick and perfunctory hug. "Though I think it's probably been since last Christmas."

"That's right," Debbie agreed affably. "I wish they had these company parties more often. I mean, I hear about all of you every day—work is all Ryan ever talks about. But he never brings me into the office—I think I embarrass him."

"No, you don't, silly!" he insisted, turning even more red.

Sheila decided not to mock them, as she usually did, and tried in earnest to be genuine.

"So, *how are you, Debbie?*" she asked, leaning in closely. Ryan eyed Sheila suspiciously. Clearly, her sincerity bothered him.

"Oh, you know. Four kids keep me busy-busy-busy," she prattled. "Always on the go—that's me!"

"I can imagine," Sheila nodded.

"You don't have kids, do you, Sheila?" Debbie asked, gingerly taking a sip of champagne.

"No, I don't."

"Oh, that is so sad!" Debbie pouted, as Ryan wrapped his arm around her, as if in warning. Debbie got the hint. "I mean, not that kids are the goal, right? Just—well, for me, I love it. But I can see how…" Debbie attempted a cheery smile, as if to erase everything she'd just said.

"I have a dog," Sheila noted, attempting some degree of communication. "Two, actually. And a, uh, friend. He couldn't make it."

"Good for you!" cheered Debbie. "See, your life is terrific, just as it is!"

"I'm—I think we need some food now, don't we, hon?" Ryan attempted a grin, which did not fool Sheila, his face now the same shade of red as the tablecloths. "A little too much of the vine!" he motioned, miming a drink. With an embarrassed nod, Ryan squeezed Debbie even tighter, steering her toward the buffet.

Sheila stood for a moment, her eyes trailing the couple, but not really seeing. Instead, she thought of Stanley, sitting at home. Was he really what she wanted? What she deserved? She'd always demanded the best, but had settled for the first man who seemed to want her. He didn't mind that she always snapped at him, or that she could unflinchingly rake a waiter over the coals, or managed to find fault in most everything. But why was that? Why did he *not* care? Surely such things as kindness matter. But not to Stanley. And she had chosen him, because with him, she didn't have to change. She didn't have to improve, as he never challenged her to do so. He was a sofa, when what Sheila really needed was a treadmill with adjustable incline.

The soundtrack of the party created a hypnotic state. Sheila was there, but her mind couldn't pull itself from the visions Debbie had inadvertently conjured. *A terrific life,* she'd insisted. Is that what Sheila had? It didn't feel terrific. Up until now, it had felt sufficient. But not in any contextual way—any way that mattered. It simply *was.* And that had been enough. Until now.

And children? There had never been any thought. Sheila knew that it wouldn't happen, ever. She'd never be a good mother; at least she was smart enough to realize that. Still, with Debbie's enthusiasm, Sheila wondered. Children would've kept her company, but she had Stanley. And the dogs. Children could've helped in her old age, fed her soup. But isn't that what nursing homes were for? Children demanded everything and provided nothing. They were a game for givers and Sheila wasn't a giver.

She was about to head for the buffet stations when it hit her. *Children bring joy.* They weren't the only source, that was true, but they were one source, and Sheila had no joy. Would she even recognize the feeling?

How sad, to be without joy. Well, not really sad. But empty. *My life is empty without joy.*

She felt others pass, nodding holiday greetings, but no one else approached. She knew she made it difficult to do so, even if one had been inclined. There was something about the way she held herself, her chin tilted up just a hair too high, which said, *Only if you dare.*

Her eyes landed on Harold, charming the gaggle of receptionists as usual. He'd bought a new suit, with a nice tailored fit. Clearly, he was expecting a decent bonus, but Sheila knew she had him beat in sales. Laughing, he raked his fingers casually through his sculpted mane with studied nonchalance. The girls leaned even closer, enraptured, as if his every word a jewel. *How dense they must be,* she thought, *to be falling for his canned patter.*

True, Sheila herself had fallen for it. Well, not the patter. She'd known he was a player from the moment they'd met, but she was okay with that. She didn't want a commitment. She wasn't looking for talk. She'd wanted sex and she got it. A lot. And there were times, even now, when Harold would catch her eye and she knew that she could have it again. But she couldn't do that to Stanley. Could she?

While Stanley wasn't what she now wanted, she had to admit he was loyal. A loyal sofa. Still, she knew she'd never betray him. It was one thing to be a single woman on the prowl and another entirely to be on the hunt once partnered. Guys could step out on their wives and receive a hearty slap on the back, but a woman was simply labeled a slut. And Sheila had worked too hard for that.

Harold looked up from his harem, connecting eyes. Sheila blushed, despite herself, and raised her glass to him. He gave a quick nod, then leaned back in to his admirers, muttering something that led to a peel of laughter.

This party had been a mistake. She should have brought Stanley—that much was clear. How could she have worked for this company for four years and have no one to talk to?

She grabbed another glass of champagne and drank quickly. It was flavorless and cheap, even for Higgins, but at the moment, that didn't much matter. She closed her eyes, hoping against hope that when she again opened them something would've changed. But the merriment around her had only increased, with everything seeming even bigger and louder than before.

Wandering through the revelers, Sheila decided on a change of scene. Pulling open the patio door, she unwittingly triggered a sharp burst of cold air.

"Shut the damn door!" someone cried, their identity obscured by the door slamming securely behind her.

She'd wanted solitude, but found there were others on the patio. A few smokers, huddled close. Normally she would've hated their smoke, but there was something about its sharp scent that contrasted nicely with the false frivolity from which she'd just escaped. She wouldn't complain.

On the far side of the patio, she spotted Nora, from the copy room, looking so small, engulfed in her dark navy pea coat, hands shoved deep into its pockets. Her pale face framed by harsh bangs, she sat with her feet up on the chair opposite, her black leggings revealing holes on both knees. Sheila couldn't believe girls today. Had they no drive? No desire for success? Before she had time to look away, Nora peered up, locking eyes. Despite their unfamiliarity, Sheila approached, needing diversion.

"Sure is cold," she offered.

Nora nodded, eyes locked on Sheila, but otherwise didn't respond. Sheila tried another tack.

"Are you enjoying the party?"

Nora just shrugged, staring at Sheila as if she could see through her skin all the way to the bone. Sheila laughed, as if Nora had said something funny or had even spoken at all. She wished the waiters were circulating with champagne on the patio as well.

"That's some red," Nora noted, finally speaking.

"Oh, thank you!" Sheila gushed, looking down at her gown. "It's Badgely Mischka. I saw it at Bloomingdales, in the window, and kept coming back to it, again and again."

"I didn't say I liked it."

Sheila's eyes narrowed. "Oh, I—uh—"

"No, it's fine," Nora interjected. "I didn't mean to be rude. It's just—very red."

Nodding, Sheila's eyes looked about, searching for someone to use as an escape. "Yes, it is red. Seemed very Christmas-y, at the time. And I like the cut."

"Hmm."

Seeing no one, Sheila decided to return inside. As much as she despised the false frivolity within, it had to be better than enduring Nora's drunken ramblings. She offered Nora a smile and "Happy holidays," before turning toward the door.

"There are other ways," Nora said, so quietly Sheila was uncertain she'd heard right. She turned.

"*Other ways…?*" Sheila parried. "Other ways for what?"

"To be."

Yes, she'd been right. Clearly, the girl had been drinking. She was young, of course, and probably hadn't learned that getting hammered at an office party easily becomes the stuff of legend.

"Hmm…" Sheila murmured, trying to be agreeable. No need to get messy with a drunk. She wrapped her arms around herself tightly, wishing she had not checked her wrap.

"Did you know I got a promotion?" Nora tilted her head forward, again engaging Sheila. "And I didn't have to sleep with anyone to get it!" Nora guffawed.

Was that dig at me? Sheila wondered. No one knew about Harold—did they?

"Congratulations," Sheila managed. "I'm sure it was well-deserved."

"It was," Nora stated, matter-of-factly. "I know my stuff. I deliver. And I'm nice to people. I smile. I smile a lot."

"Good for you." Sheila needed another drink. "Well, enjoy your evening."

"I will," Nora nodded. "I hope you do, too."

Offering a tight smile, Sheila turned toward the door, but thought she caught the evilest of tiny grins on Nora's face. Did Nora know something Sheila didn't?

Hurrying inside, Sheila was mindful to quickly close the door so as not to provoke another cry from those standing near it. Seeing the crowd gathered at the dance floor, she realized the time had come for the annual awards, which Paul Higgins took more seriously than warranted. While it was his company, you'd have thought him the King of England, the way he grandiosely announced each honoree before bestowing cheap Plexiglas trophies.

Having been head of the most profitable division, Sheila knew she'd receive something; she always did. One year she'd gotten cash, which was promptly put toward a good use: dermabrasion. Another year she received a trip to Vegas, which she'd given to her sister, Valerie, as she knew Val would appreciate the booze and smoke far more than Sheila. This year had been one of her best yet. What could Higgins give her?

She had to wait, along with everyone else, suffering through the endless corny jokes and alcohol-fueled sincerity, and found herself wishing the waiters were still circulating with champagne. She could've gone to the bar, but they'd now switched to no-host, and there was no way Sheila would pay for her own booze. She'd given too much to this company. Besides, Paul was finally getting to the big awards.

It was the usual suspects: Harold, Nick, Scotty T., and the obsequious Darrell Kingston, Sheila's not-so-friendly rival. All were praised, with shouts coming out from the crowd, who clearly were beyond buzzed.

The patio door swung open, another blast of arctic freeze blasting the banquet hall, and Sheila saw, from the hooded silhouette, that Nora had come back inside.

I smile, she'd said. *I smile a lot.*

Idiot. Sheila had known girls like her all her life. Odd, prescient, scary. A bit on the fringe. Always watching and biting their fingernails without heed…

She was glad she wasn't like that. She would've never gotten anywhere, acting that way. Now, she had a corner suite and was the envy of everyone, even if they thought her cold.

Realizing that Higgins was finally getting to her, Sheila straightened up and smoothed her hair. *These moments are to be cherished,* she told herself. *This is what it is all about.* It would've been nice to have Stanley beside her, even knowing he wasn't *the one,* if only because he alone would congratulate her in earnest.

"She's increased sales this year by over thirty-five percent," Higgins was saying. "Which is a heck of a lot better than any other division. But I always knew Sheila Mueller had more balls than any man here!"

The crowd roared and even Sheila laughed a little. She would always be judged against men, her gender a footnote to her accomplishments, no matter how grand.

"Year after year," he continued, "I keep waiting to hear from an emergency room, that one of our poor guys was injured by Sheila in an accident…"

What on earth was he talking about?

"And so," he paused, stepping back to the trophy table. "I thought this most fitting." He lifted a red cloth, revealing to the crowd a gigantic soldier nutcracker.

Gasps and cries of laughter rang through the hall, and it was all Sheila could do to steady herself. She felt someone at her side.

"Easy," Nora whispered, pushing her gently toward the stage. "Go on."

Blindly, Sheila moved forward.   Around her, a sea of laughing faces blurred, forcing her to breathe deeply as she lurched toward the stage. All she could see was red: the red of the nutcracker soldier's jacket, the red of the tablecloths, the red of Higgins' eyes…

She felt tears coming and forced them back, throwing her head back in jaunty laughter, as if this gift were all she'd ever wanted. Taking it, she leaned to Higgins, who looked startled, and hugged him to her in a strong, long kiss. Turning, she held the nutcracker above her head, showing it to the crowd and nodding along in laughter.

With a wink, she stepped off the stage, quickly making her way toward the back of the room, trophy in hand. A few felt inclined to slap her on the back, and the force from their hands felt as if they were pushing her lungs deeper into the pit of her stomach.

She continued out, with a practiced smile, nutcracker cradled in arm, past the buffet and into the ladies room. Glancing under the stalls to make sure they were empty, she proceeded into the large handicapped stall, locking the clasp firmly. She leaned back against the door, trying to get her bearings and breath. Both were slow in coming.

That this was her life suddenly seemed impossible. How had it ever gotten to this point? She'd been so focused on success, she couldn't see how much she was hated. Laughed at behind her back and, now, to her very face. *Poor Sheila, cold and uncaring. Self-centered. It's a wonder she has a man—wouldn't a dildo be enough? Look up bitch in the dictionary, and you'll see her face…*

And the terrible part was, it was true, every bit. She'd engineered all of this. This hatred. The idea that she was a heartless monster was easy for people to believe, for they'd never seen her, in all her years at the company, be any different. She'd given Higgins her all. And for what? A six-figure paycheck? That wasn't it. Money wasn't important. She wanted to be appreciated. To be taken seriously for her contributions. She'd worked her ass off for years to be valued as an equal, yet been reduced to laughing stock in less than a minute.

She looked down at the nutcracker, with its sinister stare,

teeth bared, and realized with a start that she was looking at a reflection of herself. With an intake of air, Sheila suddenly burst. Grabbing the nutcracker like a bat, Sheila swung it: at the tile wall, at the handicap rail, at herself. She swung again and again, battering the nutcracker, pieces flying and crunching underfoot, feeling a scream erupt from her lips despite herself. The roar filled the room, echoing in her ears, and she suddenly knew she had gone too far.

Looking down at her hands, now raw and tender, she saw that the nutcracker she still held no longer had a face, nor arms, nor hat. Bits and pieces were strewn about, the tile floor now a bloodied battlefield. It would be impossible to put back together; not that Sheila would try.

She dropped the remaining piece, which tumbled with a thud. Glancing about, Sheila kicked an arm out of her way as she moved to the toilet paper, pulling off a long piece. With a snort, she blew, pulling off another chunk to wipe her cheeks.

Fuck, she thought, looking at the damage. *They'll know they got to me.*

Maybe that had been their goal. Or maybe they'd thought it was all in good fun. Either way, she felt used.

Pulling herself together, she opened the stall, only to see Nora standing quietly, waiting. Sheila ignored her, moving to the basin. Pulling out some paper towels, she wet them under Nora's watchful eye. Softly, she patted down her cheeks, erasing the trails as best she could.

What is this girl doing here? Witnessing my downfall?

Sheila turned. "What, Nora? What?"

Nora stepped close, almost too close, before speaking. The room was still, putting Sheila even more on edge.

"What do you want?" Sheila asked, evenly.

Nora looked completely composed. Eerily so. "There are other ways to be," she said, just as before.

Her hand flew out so fast, Sheila wasn't even aware she'd reacted, her palm slashing flat across Nora's cheek. With a gasp, she realized what she'd done and let out a sob of horror, her hands moving to cover her cry.

Cheek on fire, Nora simply moved closer, pulling Sheila to

her, wrapping her arms tenderly, holding her. Sheila collapsed into the embrace, tears flowing freely, her body convulsing quietly as they came.

Finally, her tears stopped, but Sheila didn't move and neither did Nora. Nora just held her, solemnly, as if Sheila were a frightened child, which wasn't far from the truth.

At the basin, a faucet dripped rhythmically. Instead of annoying her, Sheila found the consistency reassuring. She allowed herself to stay, protected in Nora's arms, as a sense of calm, one she'd never known, came quietly over her.

Her eyes drifted to the nutcracker remains, scattered about; there was something about their disjointedness that reminded Sheila of her life. She'd tried to compartmentalize herself, shutting out all distractions, only to realize she needed connections. The human interaction she'd run from, viewing it as frivolous, was instead essential.

She remained in Nora's arms, who didn't seem to mind, as the faucet dripped steadily.

A noise behind told her that someone else had entered the room, and—seeing them entwined—just as quickly fled.

She didn't want others to run from her, she now knew. She wasn't a scary monster, or a bitch, or a nutcracker. She was simply Sheila, poor, confused, and unhappy Sheila, who'd made a series of ill-considered decisions, from which she was now determined to extricate herself.

After all, she reasoned with a deep sigh, *there are other ways to be.*

FESTIVE BEAVER

FESTIVE BEAVER

LITTLE RUSTY SIMS PEERED CAREFULLY at his freshly polished nails. Had he gone too far? No, he didn't think so. True, the gloss was shinier than usual, but Mardi Gras simply demanded festivity, even at Beaver Elementary. To his knowledge, his school had never before celebrated Mardi Gras, and, as he himself had suggested this merriment, Rusty knew that he must do whatever necessary to ensure its success. The other children on the Spirit Squad had little imagination and Rusty, perhaps, had too much.

For starters, none of the others had a clue as to how to even spell *Mardi Gras*, let alone a notion as to what it celebrated. Rusty, to counter their ignorance, held an emergency session of the Spirit Squad, instructing them on the finer points of the holiday. He filled their heads with visions of beautiful floats, elaborate feathery masques, and the most exquisitely detailed costumes. One dim-witted boy, Shawn "Snickers" O'Toole, mocked, suggesting that Rusty was just looking for an excuse to don a dress, but Rusty simply threw Snickers his best diva glare and went right on outlining his plans. He was used to such remarks, after all, chalking them up to jealousy.

As Rusty continued, his rhetorical skills coming deftly into play, Mrs. Braun prayed silently in the corner, hoping none of the children knew of the debauchery that was the actual Mardi Gras. Mrs. Braun had unwittingly found herself in New Orleans during the annual festivities and, caught up in the moment, was provoked into lifting her blouse. Lloyd had been with her, encouraging her brazenness. Every time she flashed someone, it inspired in Lloyd a sexual aggression the likes of which she'd never seen. Throughout their trek down Bourbon, Mr. Braun would hold her close, grinding his pelvis into her at every opportunity, as handfuls of dazzling beads were tossed from passing floats. Feeling Lloyd pressing against her, she would reach back, giving him a quick tug before presenting her breasts to the screaming masses.

Of course, Rusty knew nothing of such perversions. Instead, he innocently told a Mardi Gras tale honoring the Twelfth Night feast of the Epiphany, the day, tradition had it, the three kings first visited baby Jesus. He went on to explain that in order to pay homage to the Christ child, people put on masks, skimpy costumes, and drank far-too-much alcohol. As disinterested as the Spirit Squad was, the children knew better than to discourage any opportunity to miss class and were thus eager to go along with Rusty's plan.

Party coordination began in earnest, though not smoothly enough for Rusty. The other children tried but could not seem to master basic decorating concepts, such as "Sparkle, Sparkle, Sparkle." In one heated debate, Little Rusty seethed as the girls argued over the differences between tan, taupe, and beige. When Randall Shitsu, who would grow up to become a plumber, shouted, "What does it matter? It's all just brown anyway," Little Rusty steamed, his face flushing with anger.

That these "peers" did not understand the subtle differences in shade was understandable. But that they showed no apparent interest in even expanding their aesthetic horizons irritated Rusty to no end. In an effort to enlighten, Rusty brought in color chips and a slide show presentation entitled "Earth Tones Are Easy!," which only served to make his team less appreciative. Some even dropped out, to which Rusty shouted, "Be gone with you!"

As the weeks flew past, Little Rusty worked tirelessly, helping his krewe build their float. With Rusty's guidance, they selected *Alice in Wonderland* as their theme. The exotic and abstract float perfectly captured the magical, confusing world into which Alice fell, and Rusty knew how she must have felt: he was delirious with excitement as he saw his plans realized. He had envisioned a day of wonder and it was quickly becoming a reality. All of the hard work, planning, fighting, and biting had been worth it.

Although no one had yet hinted, Rusty felt certain that his team would vote to crown him King of Krewe, for he had been their diligent leader, inspiring them from day one and coming up with all the best ideas. True, he had occasionally been a bit of a tyrant, redoing work when it wasn't up to snuff, but he still felt confident of their admiration. Nevertheless, to ensure his nomination, he brought them fresh, warm brownies on the morning of the vote, which he'd made himself from scratch.

Fat Tuesday finally arrived, and Rusty awoke, beside himself. He had worked on his costume, a faithful rendition of Alice's Mad Hatter, for an entire month, pouring over every edition of the book he could find to ensure it was properly detailed. He sketched endlessly, creating a dizzying array of outfits until he finally settled on the perfect piece. Though somewhat hesitantly, his mother helped sew on each sequin with loving tenderness. Even before he arrived at school, however, Rusty began to suspect that all might not proceed as planned. As he carefully maneuvered his way into the minivan, dressed immaculately and fingernails glittering, a kid on a bike rode by and shouted "Pussy-boy!"

Rusty caved inside, willing the car seat to swallow him whole. As the tears started to well, however, he caught his mother's concerned eyes in the rearview mirror, quickly reading her signal: *Watch the mascara.*

Arriving at school, Little Rusty was shocked by what he saw: very few people were even wearing costumes and those that did were mainly store-bought. As the day progressed, disappointment dripped over Rusty like rain. Nothing went as planned and Little Rusty's spirit, usually buoyant, was quickly deflating. The parade was not festive so much as tiresome, overrun with Teenage Mutant Ninja Turtles and cheap, dollar store masques. Further, his krewe let him down, passing him over as King in favor of horrible Connie Hicks. After all, it had been his idea that she play Alice in the first place! His worst humiliation, though, came with the announcement that his team had lost the "Best of Parade" award to the first grade float featuring the Teletubbies.

Spirit crushed, he was determined not to show it. Somehow, he managed to hang on until the closing bell rang, releasing the children from school.

Outside, sitting forlornly on the curb, Little Rusty waited impatiently for his mother.

It was unfair. All of it. They should have won. He had worked so hard, and for what? He began ripping sequins off his costume, muttering under his breath. Was this what life was to be like? One disappointment after another?

All the emotion he'd held inside began to swell, until he had no choice but to let the tears finally come.

"Mascara be damned," he sobbed. "I want to be King!"

As he contorted his face into an unflattering masque, a shadow fell over him. Slowly, he raised his makeup-streaked face to find himself staring directly into the bright blue eyes of Joe Kimball, Beaver's all-around 6th grade stud. Joe grinned, leaning down, and wiped the black mess from Rusty's cheek.

"Hey now, Rusty—what's the matter?"

Scared that Joe was going to take the opportunity to mock, Rusty played it safe, turning his attention to the ground. Undeterred, Joe sat, draping his arm around Rusty's shoulder. As he did, Rusty felt all the blood in his body rush up to his face, as if his skin were on fire, and wondered what had prompted such a reaction.

"This isn't about the parade, is it?" Joe pressed, to which Rusty nodded. "Aw—everyone knew yours was the best! When your float rounded that corner, and I saw you there, sparkling, waving to the crowds—and that costume!—Well just, you looked—I mean, I saw you and I thought—"

"Yes…?" Rusty prompted.

"Well, to me, you're just—"

Before Joe could complete his sentence, a minivan rounded the corner with a toot, Rusty's mother waving. Spotting her, Joe blushed, then stood.

"Looks like your Mom."

"Yes," purred Rusty, as smoothly as possible. "Her timing is impeccable."

"Okay. Well, I'll see you then…" Joe said, hopefully.

Rusty offered his best Loni Anderson-smile, then, not wanting the moment to end, slowly glided over to the waiting van. With a quick peek back at the watching Joe, Rusty winked, ducking inside and smartly buckling his seatbelt. As the van pulled away, he watched until Joe was no longer in sight.

Eyeing Rusty covertly, his mother took note of the mix of joy and heartache he held within. She'd always known he was special, but also knew that the very things that made him unique would not always be valued by others.

As Little Rusty pulled out his blush and mascara, repairing the damage, his mother vowed, then and there, to faithfully shepherd him until he was able to fashion his own singular place in the world. To be sure, his mother thought, it will likely be a land filled with beauty, passion, creativity, and sly smiles between men. A place where Rusty, finally, might find himself celebrated as King of the Krewe.

THE
ROAD BACK
TO HOME

The Road Back to Home

SADIE ANNE GOT UP THAT MORNING as always, fixing her usual bowl of Post Toasties with half a banana cut into it. To this she added a bit of non-fat milk before putting the carton back into the exact same place in the fridge it always occupied. Pushing a fallen wisp of hair firmly back into place, Sadie turned to face her cat, Agatha.

"I hate leaving you. But it's only for the weekend," said Sadie, resting her hands with a sigh onto her soft, round hips. She rubbed them lightly, wondering when her hips had gotten so, well, lady-like. After all, she had only just hit 40. This wasn't supposed to happen. She worked out, zumba'd, ate low-fat, rarely drank; in fact, she'd cut just about everything pleasurable out of life in order to stave off this very moment, and it had happened anyway.

Sadie glanced at the clock: 7:38 A.M. Just enough time to feed Aggie, do a quick check of her luggage, then walk the short two blocks south to the pharmacy, then work, where she'd suffer through the last hours before her flight. It was a route she had taken many times, never varying. But today was different.

How quickly the arrival of that letter had turned her life upside down. One moment she'd been relatively content and the very next, new blood coursed through, invigorating her every move. *Is this what letting go feels like?*

Walking briskly, Sadie found that the street was alive with people going about their daily tasks. Everywhere she looked, there were people running, laughing, yelling, hailing a cab, looking in store windows... Had they been there the day previous? Were they, in fact, there every day? How could she not have noticed? For Sadie, each day was one of solitude. She was so set in her ways, so oblivious to anyone but herself, she'd come to shut out almost everything.

Turning the corner at Sixth, Sadie started to avert the newsstand so as to avoid the pornographic magazines displayed as blatantly as the lamb hung in the butcher's window. But today, instead, she stopped. Sadie looked over the beautiful home and style magazines, with their impossibly perfect photographs, took in the screaming headlines on the *New York Post* and *Daily News*, and—yes—found herself staring at the objectified women on the covers of the men's magazines.

What do those women have that I don't? Sadie asked herself.

The answer was unsatisfyingly simple. Those women were pretty, not plain. They were large breasted, not average. They were confident, not timid. And they were unafraid of their sexuality, not... Well, it wasn't that Sadie was *afraid*, exactly. She'd had sex, but it never seemed much like the type of love she read about in her novels. There was nothing romantic about it. It had been perfunctory or athletic, depending on the partner, but rarely tender, sweet, or caring.

Remembering to stop at the pharmacy, Sadie was about to cross when she suddenly stopped. As people rushed past, Sadie stood, perfectly still, and inhaled. As she did, the scent of cinnamon filled her. She closed her eyes, reminded of cherished Christmas mornings: waking up to the scent of her mother's hot cross buns baking in the oven, racing downstairs to beat Shelley to the stockings, and always, always winning. It had been important for her to win.

She regretted now how competitive she'd been. She and Shelley had once been so close, and yet now never spoke. Sadie had chosen sides, selecting blame over understanding, and that act—that cutting out—had led to the compartmentalized life she now led.

From the sparse look of her apartment, you'd never know a

holiday was fast approaching. She hadn't had the urge to decorate in years, but the arrival of the letter changed that. She suddenly found herself at the florist, splurging on a seasonal centerpiece with red candles, which seemed entirely appropriate given that a wick within, long dormant, had finally been relit.

Others might think her foolish, she knew, but Sadie discovered that she enjoyed life again. She couldn't believe she'd shut out friends and family for so long, going so far as to avoid all holidays with a vengeance. Nothing remotely warm, or caring, or loving had been allowed into her heart. As far as Sadie was concerned, a heart full could only lead to heartache. "As long as I have Aggie, I'll be just fine." And so she had been.

Until the letter.

It had come without warning, on a Tuesday. Even lying on the floor, half covered by advertisements and bills, Sadie saw the handwritten script and knew who had sent it.

She did not open it immediately. Instead, she placed the envelope carefully against her favorite Lladró—the one with the little girl leaning against the whitewashed fence—and took a hot bath.

The steam felt good against her face. She reached for the washcloth, dipping it in the dish of ice water she had put next to the tub. She quickly swathed the cloth across her face, enjoying the briskness it brought. She shivered slightly as she again dipped the cloth, refreshing her face. She luxuriated, lingered, but was in truth avoiding.

Standing, she unplugged the tub and toweled off. Sadie turned to the steam-fogged mirror with a grimace. She had forgotten to turn on the fan. The letter's arrival hadn't upset her that much, had it? She had not been expecting it, but it did not surprise her. She'd always known it was a possibility.

Sadie shivered, wrapping the robe around her. *"It's not even cold,"* she thought as she rubbed her arms, trying to keep warm. Why had the letter so put her on edge? Hadn't everything already been said, countless times before? What could the letter possibly say that would ease the pain of a life led in loneliness? Could mere words end a stalemate?

And what if the letter was *not* the expected olive branch, but a continuation? Sadie knew that she couldn't take any more of the same tired arguments and counter arguments that had consumed and diminished her life for so long.

Securing the robe at her waist and stepping into her furry slippers, she at last approached the curio cabinet, looking doubtfully at the letter before picking it up. Like a detective searching for fingerprints, Sadie inspected the envelope, hoping that the carefully written cursive might give some indication of the author's state of mind. If she could deduce it, then she wouldn't have to read it; she could put the letter aside and continue on with her life as if nothing had happened.

With a sigh, she sank into the well-worn armchair, its lace arm coverings salvaged at the last moment from Aunt Lorraine's estate sale. Sadie had no choice but to read the letter. It was an invitation, and now that this long-closed door was finally again open, she knew she must gather her pride and walk through.

Sadie opened the envelope, extracting the matching note card, and with a deep breath began to read.

The traffic on the way to LaGuardia was terrible. Sadie glanced nervously at her watch, wondering if they would make it. The cabbie caught her eye in his rearview mirror. "What time's your flight?"

"Eight thirty."

"You got plenty of time. We're minutes away."

Sadie turned again to the freeway. Ahead, brake lights and headlights combined to create a twisting candy cane. But Sadie wasn't thinking about the holidays. She wasn't thinking about the cautiously chosen gifts she carried in her canvas bag. She wasn't thinking about Aggie, alone at home. Sadie thought only of her plane's arrival and the events that would follow.

What would it be like? What would she say? Would she cry? Would she retreat into herself? Would the anger resurface? She felt vulnerable suddenly; a feeling she hadn't allowed herself to feel for years.

It had been so long that it was hard for Sadie to fathom

exactly how it could ever have veered from argument to accusations. At what point had she put up her wall? What had been so unforgiveable as to end all contact?

She'd long known her parents' marriage was troubled. She remembered the way she and Shelley had peered down the dark hallway late at night, the glow beneath the door at the end their only illumination. The low, murmured insistent rows, broken only by long pauses, told the twins everything they needed to know. They'd witnessed the way their parents tiptoed around each other, giving wide berth to the other, avoiding engagement. They'd taken note of the manner in which their parents began to speak, not to each other, but through the children.

"Sweetie, would you pass the beans over to your father?"

"I'm sure your mother would like some corn, Shelley."

They were always polite, but never warm. They kept their disagreements quiet, hidden, seeming to have agreed upon an unspoken code, allowing cohabitation without connection, which made the subsequent shock that much greater.

Why? Why now? Their parents had managed fine throughout the years, but now that the girls were out of the house, they were actually divorcing? Dad moving out? Was there no other path forward?

Shelley had taken it in stride, but Sadie was filled with anger and ache. It seemed so unfair, so selfish of her father, but her parents and sister were resolute, refusing to place blame. As they continued to try to reason with her, to explain, the solidarity between the three began to feel very much like treason. Here Sadie was, off to college and finding her way in the world, only to discover her family forever altered. She wanted to strike out—and did—at him. He'd ruined everything. Her every childhood memory was now tainted. Her father's self-centered quest for happiness had destroyed all she'd treasured.

They tried to dissuade her, to tell her she was wrong, but Sadie wouldn't listen. The split had been a long time coming, they repeatedly insisted, and completely amicable. But, to Sadie, this turn of events felt anything but amicable. She'd come to believe that all parents were like hers: quiet, polite, and plodding. She didn't know that other couples experienced joy and were happy to see each other at the end of a long day. She'd come to believe that what her parents had was ideal. Her perfect family was now shattering into a million pieces, and she was the only one who cared enough to fight for it.

She couldn't believe that Shelley didn't share in her anger, and the sudden disconnection between siblings further fueled her. She felt shunned and despised. No one could understand why she had targeted only her father for blame, and the questioning looks they gave her made Sadie feel as if *she* were the reason for such turmoil.

In that one tumultuous afternoon, just as the sun had shifted from gold to burnt orange, Sadie found herself transformed from a vibrant college freshman into the sad and bitter woman now reflected in the taxicab window.

When they were seven, Sadie and Shelley experienced the most magical of Christmases. In the days leading up to the 25th, Aunt Lorraine had taken the twins to visit Santa at the annual Eastern Star Holiday Party. Both girls squirmed so during the magic show that Lorraine had to shush them several times. At any other occasion, they would have loved the card tricks, and the disappearing handkerchief, and the funny songs, but Shelley and Sadie were focused on only one thing: Santa.

Elderly ladies passed around homemade sugar cookies and big jugs of orange punch, but that did little to calm the girls' jitters. As the women began clearing away the paper plates, Sadie was about to steal Shelley's last cookie when a commotion at the back of the room caught her attention. Everyone was standing, cheering, blocking the small girls' view.

"What's happening? What's going on?" they asked.

"It's Santa, you dolts," sneered the big red-haired boy next to them. "Don't you know Santa when you see him?"

The twins quickly turned from the frightening boy and began jumping up and down, trying to get a peek.

"Stop that, girls!" snapped an especially shrunken old woman. "Everyone will get to see Santa in time. But bad little girls don't get to see Santa. In fact, they don't get anything at all! Sit down and behave."

With a shrug and a sigh, Sadie and Shelley sat, impatiently waiting for their turn.

After what seemed like an hour, but was probably much less, it was at last their moment. Most of the other children had already left, red stocking of treats in tow, when the girls finally approached Santa. Both were a little nervous and more than a little tired when Santa reached down, pulling each onto a knee.

"Ho ho ho and a Merry Christmas to you! Now, let me see," said Santa, putting his gloved finger to his lips before gesturing to Sadie Ann. "You—you must be Sadie, and you," turning to her sister, "are Shelley, right?"

Both girls stared at each other in awe. "How—?" Sadie stammered.

"Oh, I know lots about you. You're twins, right? Just had birthdays, too."

"How do you know—?"

"And you, Sadie, are the questioning, inquisitive one, always chasing life, right? Whereas your sister here, well, Shelley, you're a bit more quiet, aren't you?—And quite the painter, from what I hear."

Shelley nodded, speechless.

"And you live with your mother and father in a nice yellow house, with your new puppy Jasmine—who you named—didn't you, Sadie?"

Sadie just stared.

"Oh, and your Aunt Lorraine, who's over there waving, she lives with you, too."

Bewildered, the girls looked over to their slightly-daffy aunt, who smiled her silly grin at them as the flashbulb went off. It was all true—every bit. They did have a dog, and a yellow house, and Aunt Lorraine had just moved into the room over the garage with all of her wonderful bundles of fabric and antique lace and giant balls of yarn.

"And I know one more thing about you both." The girls turned to him with glazed eyes. "Want to know what it is?"

The girls nodded.

"I know that your family loves you very much. No matter what. And that you'll always have a home with them, whenever you want it."

Sadie looked at her sister strangely. What did he mean? Of course their family loved them. Wasn't that what families were for? And what did he mean about having a home?

Santa hugged them close. "You've both been very good this year. So good, in fact, that I wouldn't be surprised if you each got everything you asked for."

Everything? Was he kidding? Their lists had been two pages long!

But it was true. Santa brought every item they'd requested. The dolls with the shiny blond hair and pretty blue ribbons. The Golden Books, with their bright and cheery covers and happy-ending stories. And the very grown-up bicycles with the training wheels you could take off in time.

What a wonderful Christmas they'd had. Their parents had smiled, nodding knowingly as the twins eagerly opened their gifts. Aunt Lorraine sat contentedly in the rocker, pleased with her new sewing kit from the twins. And little Jasmine frolicked and played with the discarded paper, happy to be included. Everything about that day had been ideal, and Sadie felt fortunate to be among such love.

After the gifts had all been tried out and tried on, and after the last hot cross bun had been eaten, and after the sun had gone down for the day, Sadie went to each family member and thanked them for their gifts. Thanked them for their love. And thanked them for the best Christmas of her life.

With a soft whir, the airplane door opened. Sadie sat for a moment, uncertain, and prayed for her very own happy ending. Then, canvas bag in one hand, overnight bag in the other, and coat tucked under arm, Sadie jostled with the others, emerging nervously from the plane. She stared at the crowd gathered at the gate, searching for a familiar face.

Suddenly, she found it. The face was a little rounder than she remembered, and the eyes a bit dimmer—but they were welcoming. So welcoming, though, and filled with such love and forgiveness, that Sadie—sad and bitter and lonely Sadie—began to cry.

And as she did, Sadie found herself slowly moving toward those eyes. Toward the love. Toward the caring. Toward her father's arms stretched out, open wide.

It was then that she saw it.

Held gently, in one wrinkled and weathered hand, was a faded red felt Santa hat, with a bit of cotton glued stiffly at the top.

THE
STEPPING
STONE

THE STEPPING STONE

LOOKING AT HIS PALE, THIN TORSO lit by the unforgiving fluorescents, Gerald frowned. His brittle arms hung limply at his sides and his sharply drawn face seemed composed only of triangles. In all, there was something about his naked physique that reminded him of a plucked turkey. Turning sideways, his gut jutted forth insistently, and it was clear to Gerald that his mother's plan was succeeding.

Lolly had been clear from the beginning: she saw no career prospects for her son, given his interests in *Star Wars, Star Trek,* comic books, Japanese anime, and precious little else. She could see no path forward for him, other than one she herself orchestrated. While Gerald generally agreed that he lacked social graces and professional skills, having long been below average in all respects, there was something about his mother's machinations that reminded him of Jabba the Hut. And when Gerald really thought about it, the similarities didn't end there.

His mother had always been corpulent, and her lumbering appearance at school events had filled him with shame ever since he could remember. But, while embarrassed by her size, it was her demeanor that irked him most. Lolly lacked faith in him, and in all of humanity, both of which she found continually disappointing.

Still, when she first learned that the mall was hiring, Gerald had been optimistic. It was a stepping stone, she'd said, surely to lead to bigger and better things. And, the first season in the role, he allowed himself to believe it. It would be dealing with the public, challenging and improving his skills, but with a level of remove the costume allowed. And it would be easy, he figured, to simply sit in a chair and wave. But being the Easter Bunny turned out to be more difficult and less entertaining than he'd anticipated.

He was not allowed to hop out to his throne in the photo area; it was mandated that he walk, his hand held firmly by any of one of the part-time girls unattractive enough to have been denied employment by the mall's hundred or so fashionable retail establishments. *Hopping* had been deemed an insurance liability as well. There was also an underlying fear that, mid-jump, he might somehow trip, sending his gigantic head rolling off and scaring the waiting line of children, which apparently had happened before.

In truth, there was never much of a line and it was easy for Gerald to see why. The feeble Easter Bunny offerings could in no way match that of Santa Claus. Kids looked forward to seeing Santa, to impart their holiday wishes, ask questions, or simply to get their annual photo taken. With the Easter Bunny, the children generally didn't have anything to say. They'd sit, dutifully, and smile, but Gerald never received anything like "Hey, Easter Bunny, what are you gonna bring me this year?" as all knew the answer was "Eggs." Not much mystery or surprise. At most, Gerald would get an "Aww, you're so cute!," to which he'd nod or pat the kid's shoulder.

Not that he could have responded any other way. Unlike Santa, Gerald wasn't allowed to speak. Whereas the voice of Santa could be replicated, with his bellowing "ho-ho-ho's," no one quite knew what the Easter Bunny sounded like, and management was against the idea of Gerald talking, no matter how many different character voices he auditioned for them.

The biggest difference between the roles was that, with Santa Claus, the essence of the person playing the part still came through, despite the beard, padding, and round glasses. Much could be communicated by the way the actor moved, spoke, laughed, raised his eyebrows, or smiled, whereas Gerald was saddled with a wire-framed helmet, through which he could see dimly through the darkened eye screens, the only light coming from its nostril holes. It was easy to get depressed in the suit, which tended to accentuate his ongoing feelings of inadequacy.

After only a few hours on the job, Gerald's hope that this would become, as Lolly said, a "stepping stone" was pretty much dashed. He'd already been thrown up on—twice—and watched as a young girl ate her own boogers. Still, Lolly was hopeful.

"It's the first day," she'd said. "It'll get better—mark my words. Pretty soon you'll own that mall."

While Gerald knew this would not be the case, there was little else he could do but trudge on. He made it through that season, and the next, and the next, until he had three seasons of Easter under his belt, which was beginning to feel increasingly tight. Lolly had begun to fatten him up to better his chances of becoming Santa Claus. Though still too young for the role, Gerald merely shrugged. It did no good to argue with her. Lolly had found him his first and only job thus far, which was much better than his own track record.

The problem was, there wasn't much he liked to do. Add that to his few admirable qualities and even fewer skills, and about the only work for which he qualified was janitorial in nature, which simply would not do for Lolly. She did, as she liked to say, *"have standards."* And so she continued to support her son, from one spring to the next, plying him with rich, fatty foods, in preparation for phase two of her plan.

While Gerald didn't especially want to be fat, he didn't feel as if he had much choice. After all, becoming Santa as well would mean that instead of being employed for only three weeks a year, he could add on an additional six. To keep both jobs, though, the trick would be to become large enough for Santa, but still thin enough to be the Easter Bunny. It was odd, really, because when Gerald thought about bunnies, they all came with a full, rounded silhouette. The costume, however, was very trim, as if all rabbits were emaciated like Bugs Bunny.

And so he began his fourth spring season, thirty pounds heavier than his first, and found himself in the bleakly lit break room with its fidgety vending machine when Amy walked in. She eyed him suspiciously, standing there in his rabbit suit, holding his head with one hand and a Snickers bar in the other.

"Nice," she pronounced, but there was something about the way she stretched out the word, her voice arching high on the *"I,"* that made Gerald certain she hadn't meant it as friendly. Still, he couldn't help but notice how smooth her skin looked, or the bewitching green of her eyes, or the wink she gave him as she headed into the women's locker room. Smiling to himself, he put his bunny head back on and hopped out to the photo area, management be damned.

It was a week before he next saw her, heading for the food court in her red, blue and yellow Hot Dog on a Stick uniform. *At least we have that in common,* he thought. *Ugly costumes.*

From talking to Jose, the counter help at Sbarro, he quickly learned her name—Amy, that she was five years younger—a senior in high school, and that she only worked weekends. Which meant, as Easter was quickly approaching, Gerald had only one more weekend to make an impact—or at least a more positive impression than his first.

Gerald knew better than to share anything about Amy with Lolly, as she would poo-poo any prospect of love. From his earliest years, he could remember her words and sayings hanging over him, slightly dampening his heart. Yet she always delivered them as if she were being helpful, with the two of them co-conspirators of some sort.

"You know, love, that math isn't your best subject! Or science. Or—. Hmm… Well, gee! Guess you can't have everything!"

"It's you and me, kid, til the day we die," she'd grin. "Who else would have us, right?"

"Lord knows you didn't inherit my smarts, but I'm sure God gave you something! It's our job to figure out *what.*"

"It's terrible, really, the way your face turned out, but you'll grow into your looks, some day," she'd chuckle. "That's what prayer is for!"

It was as if, with every remark, she was giving both smile and slap. It was odd, really, to live with someone, to have been born of them, to have someone so close, and yet feel as if they hated you. Lolly was never out rightly mean; instead, she coated each bullet with a titter, as if she didn't mean it. Still, Gerald felt certain that she did.

Before meeting Amy, he thought this was to be his destiny: Lolly, the occasional job, and his bedroom, where he ate, read, slept, and stayed. Stepping out from his room was reserved only for bathroom breaks or a quick dart to the kitchen or front door. He rarely engaged Lolly, though she would go to great lengths to zero in on him. She was constantly offering food, or a bit of news, or the offer of a backrub. But as time went on, Gerald, who had once acquiesced to her every request, found himself saying *no* much more often.

And Lolly noticed.

The next Saturday, Gerald arrived at the mall at 8:00 A.M., though Amy didn't usually get there until 9:30. He wanted to ensure that there was no possibility of missing her, and so he sat in his car, near the entrance, binoculars at his side.

Conscious of his previous attire, Gerald had taken great pains in his appearance. He'd woken, in the middle of the night, to clandestinely iron one of his few clean button-down shirts. After returning to a fitful sleep, he envisioned several different scenarios in which he'd best connect with Amy, but none felt exactly right. Finally, at 7:00 A.M., he showered, shaved, put on after-shave, and even did 10 push-ups, which felt a little bit like victory. He did all of this quietly, in order not to wake his mother. He had no idea that Lolly had lain rigid, eyes open, staring at the ceiling, listening to every creak and moan the old house made. He couldn't fool her, for Lolly was a sly one.

Once she'd noticed the change in his demeanor, she immediately took to root out its cause. It bothered her to no end that Gerald had changed—or rather—that something out of her control was changing him, leaving her in the cold. She had a right to know what was happening, she reasoned, and one morning waited, until he'd left for work, to strike.

Peering out the window, she watched as his taillights disappeared, then quickly headed into the kitchen. Pulling open the door to the laundry room, she rummaged about, reemerging with a pair of rubber cleaning gloves. Slipping them on, she tiptoed to Gerald's door, though there was no reason to do so.

Inside, the air of the room was sour, and the scent of something strong—was it pizza?—filled the air. Resisting the urge to open the window, Lolly surveyed Gerald's room. It was just as she'd expected: clothes, shoes, and silly comic books strewn about the floor, his trashcan overflowing with crumpled papers and soda cans, and a thin layer of dust coating the dresser and TV set. Again resisting the urge, this time to clean, Lolly skillfully stepped through the mess, careful not to disturb a thing.

Quietly, she opened each dresser drawer, lifting the clothes and searching with her fingers, like a sieve combing through sand. Aside from some loose change and three dog-eared Playboy magazines, the dresser had been a bust.

Crossing to the closet, Lolly slowly pulled out the hinged shutters, fearing God-knows-what could suddenly come tumbling forth. But the closet was relatively bare. It seemed that most everything previously contained within currently blanketed the carpet, creating a patchwork quilt of clothing. Rifling through the few shoe boxes on the top shelves, Lolly was disappointed to find nothing but shoes. She felt through pants and jacket pockets, picked up and examined every t-shirt, sniffing each, hoping to detect a lingering scent, until she picked up a hand-towel which she was fairly certain had been abused.

Her hunt seemed to be in vain until, underneath the bed, Lolly finally struck gold. She discovered several spiral notebooks, bound together with thick rubber bands. Gerald had never been a particularly good student, so it wasn't likely that he'd saved homework.

Pulling out one from the bottom, she opened it, and was astonished to find herself facing one of the most beautiful pencil drawings she'd ever seen. She wasn't sure what it was, exactly, but it looked quite futuristic in nature. Some kind of unique creature; half-animal, half-human. But what really took her breath away was how life-like it was. Staring into its eyes, Lolly almost felt threatened, as if this beast could leap from the page, taking her down in one swoop.

Flipping through the binders, she found more and more images. Some were just quick sketches, but others were so detailed they could have been hung in a museum. Certain pages, Lolly averted her eyes, as there were drawings of enlarged genitalia, of both genders, with people and creatures involved in all manner of unspeakable activity. And yet, mixed between the filth were pages of unfathomable beauty: lush gardens, with flowers, and magnificent structures. Imperial kings and monsters of every kind. One sketch, of an old and large woman, staring directly at the viewer, giving them the finger, even looked suspiciously like Lolly.

She pored through each, mystified that these had been crafted by her son. How could Gerald be the source for both such splendor and depravity? He'd never shown the slightest proclivity toward art, nor any other form of creativity for that matter. And, even if these were his creations, why had he kept them hidden? *It would have saved me years of worrying,* Lolly admitted to herself. *He actually has a marketable skill, after all. Just think of the money we could make!*

Lolly put such thoughts aside, as tailoring a career plan for Gerald would have to wait. Knowing now just how much he had kept hidden, Lolly was determined to discover the source of his sudden and unwelcome happiness. It wasn't that she didn't want him to be happy, exactly, but she wanted to be the inspiration for such happiness. It was disquieting to think that some*one* or some*thing* had found a way to intervene, allowing a sinister cloud to hover above their previously happy existence.

Picking up the final spiral, Lolly immediately soured. Drawn on the front was an elaborate heart, out of which poured music notes, hot dogs—even a bunny. She was very confused, for Gerald had never been the sentimental type. The matter became clear when she saw what was inside. Page after page of a woman—the same woman. Or girl. Lolly wasn't quite sure. The image was youthful, but there was something stylized about the way she'd been drawn that made her feel a little too coquettish; indeed, she looked more than a bit slutty. While some poses were simple and casual, in others she was dressed in what looked like leather, or with devil ears, or bearing a whip. In one, she was doing something awful with a corndog.

Lolly put down the books with a sigh. She'd known that this day would come, eventually, but that didn't mean she liked it. After all, most girls were irritating and Lolly knew Gerald wasn't bright or interesting enough to keep their focus for long. But this one—Gerald was clearly transfixed and it would have to be dealt with.

Restacking the notebooks in the order in which they'd been found, Lolly bound them. Surveying the room, which looked just as it had when she'd entered, Lolly felt confident her intrusion would not be noticed and quickly scurried out to begin crafting a plan of her own.

As he sat in his car, waiting for Amy, Gerald knew none of this. He was so focused on the employee entrance, not wanting to miss his beloved, that he never saw his mother's battered Oldsmobile enter the lot and park on the periphery, some distance away.

It was nearing 9:30 A.M., when both he and Amy were expected, but she still hadn't shown. Gerald felt a growing sense that something was wrong, that she wasn't coming. And so it was with relief that he suddenly spotted her, pulling her silver Hyundai into a shaded spot and installing her car sunblock above the dash. He noticed her checking her makeup, and as she pulled out lipstick, carefully applying it to her puckered mouth, Gerald couldn't help but wish that the tube were him. As she stepped from her car, Gerald did the same. He was hoping to make their meeting look casual, sauntering toward the entrance as nonchalantly as he could. As they got closer, someone behind called out "McAllister!" and Gerald felt a firm hand clamp down upon his shoulder.

"Saw you coming in—cutting it a bit late, are we?" Tony grinned as Gerald turned toward him. While irritated at having his plan interrupted, he was also nervous to see his boss as the cause. They rarely spoke and when they did it was usually because Gerald had done something wrong.

"Aww—I still have plenty of time," Gerald whined. Out of the corner of his eye, he saw Amy enter the break room and tried to steer Tony toward it. "The costume doesn't take that long."

"I'm just joshin' you, McAllister," snorted Tony. "Relax!"

"Yeah," attempted Gerald, "I knew that." He stared toward the break room, knowing it held both Amy and the entrances to the locker rooms. In one, Amy would be changing, and he should be in the other. He glanced at the clock behind Tony, wishing he'd get to the point.

Seeing his eyes dart to the time, Tony turned to him. "Forget about the kids, McAllister. Who cares if the Easter Bunny is a little late? It gives their folks more time to shop!" he laughed, though he wasn't remotely funny.

Gerald smiled, because he knew he should, and waited.

"What I'm thinking, kid, what I wanted to talk to you about, is *Christmas.*" Gerald stood, nodding, as he counted the minutes ticking by. Amy needed to be at the food court soon, leaving him little time to act. "I know you wanna be Santa," Tony continued. "You've made that clear from day one. And I gotta admit, I thought it would be years before you'd be ready. But you've impressed me, truly. The skills you've brought to the Easter Bunny..." Gerald had no idea what Tony was talking about. Skill? He sat there, dead as a doornail, and sometimes waved. "And all of those funny voices you've done for us— Wow."

"Thank you, Mr. Ferraro," Gerald said, nonetheless. "I'm glad you're pleased."

"And skinny! Boy, when you first walked through the door, I thought, no way! Unh huh—No Santa for McAllister. But today..." With a smile, Tony gestured, as if Gerald's belly had won an award. "Just look at you!"

Gerald tried to smile. This was what he'd wanted, after all. What he'd worked for. And here it was, being offered to him on a silver platter. Lolly would be so pleased. Then it hit him. None of this had been what *he* wanted. This dream had been Lolly's, right from the start. Even as he shook Tony's hand and headed toward the break room, he felt his stomach turn. While Gerald had no grand vision for himself, nor any idea of what he *wanted* to be doing, fattening himself up just to be Santa Claus was not it.

Amy stepped from the women's locker room, bobby-pinning her hat, and almost collided with him.

"Sorry!" she squeaked. "My bad!"

Gerald stopped her. "Wait!"

She looked at him square on, expectantly. While Gerald may not have known what he wanted to do with his life, it was clear, as he looked at her, that he wanted Amy.

"I'm Gerald," he managed.

"Yeah, I know." she said, smiling. "The Easter Bunny, right?" Amy laughed, connecting the dots.

"Yes," Gerald said, ducking his head. He wasn't certain if her laugh was playful or mocking, but either way, he liked the sound of it.

"Wow—that means you only have one more week's worth of work, huh?"

"Yep," he nodded. "And you only work weekends?"

"If it were up to me, I'd work every day. I love it," she smiled. "But my parents—well, they're strict about a work/life balance and homework and shit." Even the way she said "shit" Gerald found appealing.

"Could—um?" Gerald stuttered, trying to find the words to ask her out.

Amy glanced at the clock and Gerald knew his moment was passing. "Would you like to go out with me?" he asked.

She looked at him, surprised, and was about to respond when a call rang out.

"Yoo-hoo, hon!" Gerald spun about, to see Lolly standing behind, bagged lunch held high. "You forgot something!"

Incensed, Gerald stepped toward Lolly, only to see Amy shrug and grin, darting off toward her job with a wave. Lolly had ruined his moment.

"What are you doing here, Mom?" he mumbled crossly, attempting to remain calm.

"I just thought you'd be hungry," she smiled sweetly, swinging the bag in front of him.

"You know I don't bring my lunch!" He could feel heat rising from his skin, his face flushing in anger.

"That was *before* your big promotion," Lolly laughed, gaily. "Only a few more months before your debut!"

"How—?" Gerald's confusion quickly cleared as he put the pieces together. Lolly had engineered his first job and would engineer his last.

Abruptly turning on his heels, Gerald walked away, slamming the men's door behind him.

For a moment, Gerald waited, half expecting his mother to follow. Catching his breath, he could not believe what a dunce he'd been. All these years, he'd followed his mother's orders, her every wish, simply to make her happy. What about his own happiness? Had he ever had it? Or had Lolly snuffed it out, like a candle flame between two fingers?

Gathering himself, he quickly dressed, determined to be the best damn Bunny imaginable. Lolly may have gotten him the job, and even orchestrated the promotion, but Gerald alone could create success or failure. He had that in his power, and he knew he had something to prove: to Lolly, to Amy, and, most of all, to himself.

Later that night, Gerald opened the front door as quietly as he could. Peering into the living room, he saw that all lights were on, which was odd, but the house felt quiet. Seeing lights on in the kitchen as well, Gerald silently crossed toward it. Stepping in, he found Lolly, dressed nicely, sitting at a set table. She'd used the nice silver and even opened a bottle of wine, though she never drank. She hadn't heard him come in, but looked up, noticing him, and smiled.

"There you are!" she tottered, as if they hadn't experienced anything out of the norm.

Gerald stood, staring at her. *This is the woman who has made my life miserable,* he thought. *My mother. My only living relative. And all she wants is for me to be unhappy.*

Something on his face must have registered with Lolly, as she immediately changed tact.

"I was only trying to help, dear," she admitted. "You would've never gotten that job without a little nudging. I was hoping we could celebrate!"

He stood, stalk-still, and his silence—his strength—scared her.

"Was I wrong to do that?" Lolly asked, confused that her efforts had not been inspiring. *He should be grateful,* she figured.

Gerald simply turned, leaving his mother alone at her table, and went into his room, closing the door firmly behind.

Lolly sat, her blood beginning to boil. She'd been directly and resolutely shut out by her child, for whom she'd done everything. Who was this harlot who had him so smitten? How could she have so quickly enraptured him, leading him to rebuke his own mother? She must be dealt with—that much seemed clear. The question was, *how?*

Gerald was up half the night, determining how best to proceed, and had come up with a plan. It was simple, clean, and seemed foolproof. He packed up some clothes, toiletries, and the money he'd hoarded from his annual job, which turned out to be quite a lot, as Lolly had always paid for everything. But he knew he couldn't count on that anymore, and wouldn't have wanted to anyway.

Creeping outside at 3:00 A.M., he put the things into his trunk, closing it as quietly as he could. Looking up toward the house, he saw a curtain shift, ever so slightly, and knew he was being watched.

More determined than ever, he walked back inside, calmly turned off his light, and went to bed.

The next morning, Gerald awoke with a start to realize he'd overslept. After a speed shower, he was off, leaving Lolly and house receding in his rearview mirror. Just a few minutes later, however, Lolly herself emerged from the house, and the look on her face was one that would've scared a cat. Checking her rather large bag, which matched her outfit perfectly, she patted something within with what looked almost like affection.

Pulling into the mall lot, Gerald saw that Amy's car was already parked, sunblock up as usual, and knew he wouldn't have much time before her shift began. Running inside, he took great care with the wrapped package tucked under arm, as if it were fragile as glass. But Amy was already at work, leaving Gerald's only option to intersect her on break. He placed the package carefully in his locker, dressed, and began his trek out to the photo area. He didn't see Lolly, sitting some distance away, obscured by a rather large sunhat and dark glasses. But she saw him.

The line that day seemed endless; partly due to the encroaching holiday and partly as Gerald's thoughts never really left Amy. While in his mind he saw them together forever, what he really wanted, more than anything, was a date. A simple meal or coffee at which they could talk, shedding ridiculous costumes, work, and problems far behind. After all, he wasn't even sure if they were, in fact, like-minded. For example, what kind of music did she listen to? While he had a hard time envisioning her singing along to pop, it wasn't outside the realm of possibility either. She could be into rock, or emo, or even blues, for all he knew. There was an element of retro about her, which led him to believe her musical tastes would somehow surprise, but until they talked, face-to-face, he couldn't know for sure.

Gerald had never experienced the slightest discomfort wearing the bunny suit, but today he did. It was itching and constricting, and he couldn't wait to get out of it. He realized that was the same feeling that he'd felt that morning, just before leaving Lolly's. He'd been trapped, all these years, lulled into obedience, but the simple idea that something more was possible gave him hope, fueling his desire to smash the chains and, once and for all, set himself free.

At break time, Gerald quickly shed his skin, neglecting his meal, and ran to the food court, package carefully tucked under arm. It was peak time for lunch, but Gerald knew this was his only chance. It was now or never.

Lolly was there as well, eyeing him over a magazine, from which her dark round sunglasses protruded, accentuating her mammalian features. She watched as he approached Hot Dog on a Stick and noted how nervous he was. Gerald eyed the long line, then tried to catch Amy's eye, but she and her co-worker were oblivious. Lolly saw him circle about the stand, trying to find a way to make contact, before glancing to the clock hanging inside. He had little time to make his move and Lolly noted confidently that he would likely choke, simple as that, relieving her of the need to intervene.

Knowing his time was limited, Gerald was undeterred, and shoved his way past the line of people.

"Hey!" someone shouted. "We've been waiting!"

Gerald ignored the man, instead calling out, "Amy!" Startled, she turned, almost spilling the lemonade she'd been filling.

"What are you doing here?" she hissed. "I could get fired!"

He shook his head, as if he knew better. "I just need a minute. Please!"

Amy exchanged glances and shrugs with the other counter girl, then motioned. "Go down the hall. First door on your left." He virtually ran to it, waiting for her to unlock it from within. The minute she opened it, he stepped in, shutting it behind.

They stood for a moment, neither quite sure where this was going. The kitchen area was warm, and the din of the crowd just on the other side could still be heard, making their already urgent moment even more urgent.

"Yes…?" she led. "What was so important?"

"I—You're only here today. Then you're not back until next weekend, and I'll be gone," he noted insistently.

"Okay. So?"

He sighed. She wasn't making this easy. But then he realized his conversations with her had always been, until now, in his head. She wasn't privy to his thoughts and how most revolved around her. She didn't know that he had his car packed up—ready to go where, he wasn't quite clear. But he knew he had to tell her.

"I—I think I'm—" he stuttered.

"I have to get back to work," she urged.

Gerald couldn't think of the right words to say. It seemed a lifetime with Lolly had drained his every ounce of courage. Instead of talking, he thrust the package he'd been holding awkwardly into her hands.

"A present?" she managed. "Whatever for?"

"Just open it," Gerald managed, conscious that time was ticking quickly past.

Amy unwrapped it, revealing a beautiful portfolio. "But—"

He motioned for her to continue. Unlatching the clasp, she began looking through the pages, at the pictures of her, each more unique than the last.

"I—Is this me?" Amy was in awe. No one had ever done anything like it. There were drawings of her on horseback, as a warrior, fairy, dancer, and more, all in fantastically ornate settings. She motioned to one. "Is that me as Princess Naboo?"

Gerald was amazed that she knew his favorite *Star Wars* character. "Yes," he smiled. "Do—do you like it?"

She couldn't even respond. It seemed overwhelming. Here he'd been, in the same mall, watching her, and yet she had barely noticed him. It was a lovely gesture and there was something about his timidity and artistry that made her want to know him better. She looked up into his eyes and what she saw there startled her: if you could envision him without the extra weight, he was actually quite handsome.

Reaching up, she gave him a quick kiss on the cheek. "Can we meet for dinner tomorrow? My treat!"

Gerald could barely believe his good fortune. "I—uh—Sure!" he smiled.

She turned, stashing the portfolio on the supply rack. "Sorry to art and run, but I need to get back!"

He nodded, realizing that he was already late for his post. Turning, he left, back out the hallway to the food court. Both he and Amy emerged, only to face Lolly, hat and glasses off. She stood next to the waiting line of customers, and spoke, addressing both them and the line.

"Here they are!" she bellowed. "My son—and his harlot..."

No one knew just quite to make of her, but Gerald felt himself sinking within. He had no idea what she was up to, but he knew Amy would likely not be interested in someone with a mother such as his. He tried to stop her.

"Mother..." he hissed.

Lolly ignored him, instead approaching the counter and

leaning in toward Amy, who was trying her best to ignore her and focus on her waiting customer.

"Sweet talk you, did he?" Lolly grinned. "Show you his drawings?" Though talking amiably and quietly, there was nothing remotely charming about Lolly. "Pretty, aren't they? You probably felt all special, knowing of his little crush on you."

Amy turned to her customer. "Just the lemonade?" Instead of answering, the customer took a good look at Lolly and backed quickly away. Amy turned, to see what had repelled her customer, only to find herself staring at a large drawing of herself, doing intimate things with a corndog.

"Oh my God—"

Lolly laughed, turning about so that everyone around her could see the picture, which she'd had enlarged. She nodded toward Gerald, "He seems so innocent, doesn't he? All doe-eyed and sad. Pathetic really. Still, I could see how you might feel sorry for him. Bet you'd even date him, huh? Except for this."

She continued to display the image and was gathering quite a crowd. Amy whispered to her co-worker, "Get security."

Gerald stood, somewhat helpless. His every hope, his window of freedom, seemed to be closing. And it was all his doing. He'd allowed his desire for Amy to morph into a weapon, designed solely for him.

"You're crazy, Mother." The words came so quietly, they were almost inaudible. But Lolly heard them. She turned, quite quickly.

"Come with me. We're going home."

"No, we're not," he replied, as calmly as he could. "I'm not going with you. I am not coming home. Ever again."

The words were like shrapnel and the cry Lolly uttered as she sunk to her knees filled the food court, echoing out in ripples. Falling down, sobs wracked her large frame, but no one made a move to help her.

Gerald looked to his mother, then to Amy. Amy's eyes were on his, locked, and he nodded to her. "How about we make that date right now instead?"

Nodding, Amy backed into the kitchen area, reemerging

from the hallway with the portfolio in hand. Lolly had repulsed her, but there was something about the way Gerald responded that made Amy think there might be more to him than she'd imagined. He'd been chivalrous and kind, and that strength needed to be rewarded. Besides, even if Lolly had meant to scare her with that erotic drawing, it only served to make Gerald infinitely more intriguing.

Lolly looked up, her face streaked with tears and makeup, just as Amy reached out, taking Gerald's hand. They walked away, never looking back. The job she'd envisioned as a stepping stone had indeed been just that, but instead of bringing her and Gerald even closer, it had proven a toe-hold to a path that would only take him further and further away.

Pulling herself up from the ground, she glanced around at all of the people staring. She had no idea what to do or where to go.

With a resigned sigh, she turned back to the abandoned counter girl. "Gimme a corndog." And she was given one, immediately. On the house.

GLENBOURNE, IL

GLENBOURNE, IL

IT WAS A SMALL TOWN with few memorable attributes.
Kelman's Grocery Store was little more than a tiny market with
one shelf of fresh produce. The post office had one clerk
window and one staffer, in addition to the two mailmen, which
meant that if Mrs. Hellner was sick, the office stayed closed,
mail deliveries be damned. Glenbourne, IL, was far enough
south from Chicago that suburban expansion hadn't touched it,
which left it quiet, if lacking in modern features. There wasn't
much in Glenbourne to attract visitors, though those who chose
to stop could always stay at the Glenbourne Manor Guest
House, which was rather grandly named, given its basic white
farmhouse design and the fact that it rarely held more than two
guests at any one time.

The high school closed a few years back, with students now
bussed to the neighboring county, but otherwise life in
Glenbourne had changed little in the past 20 years. In fact, as
Glenn pulled down the main street, visions of his distant youth
played out before him as if they'd occurred just yesterday. The
long ride into town on his bike on a hot summer's day with just
a dollar in his pocket. Standing at the faded Sherman's Ice
Cream freezer, half frosted over, debating between the orange
Creamsicle and the ice cream sandwich. Kelman's Grocery
Store was still there, though Glenn knew from his last visit that
the old freezer had since been replaced with one storing Haagen
Dazs. Glenn couldn't imagine many here willing to pay for such

an upscale treat, but if that change meant that good things could still be found in his old home town, he wouldn't complain.

The elementary school had changed color, but otherwise looked the same. He could remember how safe he'd felt back in his youth, having no knowledge of the world and how challenging life could be. *Not insurmountable,* he often said. *If there is no hope, I'd rather hang it up.*

But with hope, Glenn felt certain he could conquer anything. Almost.

Sarah instinctively placed her hand on his knee, as if interpreting his thought, and again he felt hope. They were still a mile out from his mom's, which gave him time to reflect on the jewel sitting beside him. *I am so fortunate,* he thought, his hand covering hers with a warm squeeze.

Try as he might to be objective, he couldn't quite see what she'd seen in him. Glenn would've easily passed himself right by. But Sarah had seemed certain, content even, from their very first meeting. "You're a good person," she'd noted. "And my instincts are never wrong." That had been five years ago, and she'd seen him through so many life moments he'd begun to lose track. There had been the wedding, of course, held exactly 365 days after they'd met. His father's death just a few months later. His lay-off from the firm and their consequent move to and reinvention in California. And the recent cancer scare, which had shaken him, but had left Sarah unfazed. "If it is part of God's plan," she would repeat, "it's useless to worry."

While Glenn didn't share Sarah's deep love for the Lord, he knew better than to argue, and she knew better than to push him. He respected her faith and wished he felt the same, but all he could think about were those times as a child when he'd prayed fervently for God to cure him, only to be greeted by silence.

Sarah had been so wonderful, so complete a partner, Glenn's only regret was that they hadn't had children. He knew that while he had doubts about his own ability to parent, Sarah would excel enough for both.

The turn for his mother's drive appeared on the horizon and Sarah immediately checked her hair. She still felt a need to impress his mother, which was an urge that Glenn himself felt as well. There was something about Harriet, or Mother Burke, as she preferred to be called, an air of superiority, which demanded respect. Though Mother Burke was never fearful or mean, Sarah wasn't the first to have submitted to her and certainly wouldn't be the last.

"I wish she'd at least let me make something," Sarah sighed as they turned up the drive. "It feels weird, walking in empty-handed."

"You know Mom," Glenn grinned. "She's got to have her finger in every pie—and her arm up every turkey."

Sarah nodded, resigned. It was easier to give in than to spend countless hours shopping, prepping, and baking, only to have your handiwork dismissed with a grimace. Sarah had time, she reasoned, to find something suitable to contribute to the feast, and the bonus was that such a quest would supply plenty of excuses to journey out from the house.

When they pulled in, Mother Burke was already on the porch, fists on hips, as if barring entry to her own home. "Well there you are," she said, stating the obvious. "I was wondering what you two were up to!"

Glenn went, almost childlike, enfolding himself into his mother's waiting arms. She squeezed him tight. "How's my baby?" she sighed. "My precious baby... You look thin."

He laughed, "I'm great, Mom. Just, you know—"

Sarah stepped forward, arms conveniently and purposely full, and kissed Mother Burke on the cheek.

"Hey Harriet, good to see you," she offered, quickly moving inside and into the room she and Glenn always used. The screen door swung shut with a clatter.

After Sarah was deep within, Mother Burke noted, simply as fact, "She hates me."

"Aw, Mom, don't start."

"You always say she'll warm up, but you'd think after five years we'd at least be a step closer to tepid."

Glenn picked up their bags. "I'm not doing this," he stated, firmly but gently, moving inside and kissing her cheek as well. "And neither are you," he laughed.

After they were settled, Glenn and Sarah converged in the kitchen, as they always did.

"Wine?" he smiled.

"You read my mind," Sarah sighed. And it was true, in a way. While Mother Burke may have had issues with her, Sarah and Glenn were united, with words used almost as afterthought. It was that way during their first blind date and had been ever since.

He reached into the fridge, pulling out the Chardonnay they'd picked up on their way from the airport, knowing it unlikely Mother Burke would have anything alcoholic in the house aside from cooking wine. Glenn fumbled through a drawer before retrieving an opener. Gazing at Sarah affectionately, he began pulling out the cork when she looked up, catching his bemused smile.

"What?"

"I can't get over how beautiful you are."

As Sarah blushed, he handed her a glass. "You are some sweet talker…"

"Oh yeah?" he grinned. "What's it gonna get me?"

"Stop!" she laughed, knowing Mother Burke was likely listening to their every word. She decided to change the topic. "When does Carly arrive?" she asked.

"Oh, you know Carly—"

"Whenever she wants!" they laughed together.

"She's bringing Tommy," Glenn noted, with special emphasis, "*and* his kids."

"Kids?" Sarah was surprised. "Wow…" She let the thought linger. "Well, that'll make for a change. Usually it's just us."

"It will be nice," Glenn agreed.

There was something about an adults-only family gathering that, to him, felt rather sad. Prior to Tommy, Carly had never wanted kids, and the revolving door of disappointments she brought to each gathering had made that decision seem wise. But everything changed when Carly met Tommy. Maybe it had been the idea of giving birth that had turned Carly off. Maybe the typical maternal urges had never surfaced. Regardless, meeting Tommy, who already had three kids of his own, forever altered the equation. Carly, who had never met a barstool that didn't fit, now found herself chauffeuring his trio all over town and seemed quite thrilled to do so. Perhaps she'd grown tired of the life she'd been living and realized she wanted something different, but more likely, the right situation landed directly in her lap and Carly—for once—had done nothing to screw it up.

Mother Burke joined them in the kitchen, but while she pulled out a chair and set down her lemonade, she herself never actually sat. Instead, she busied herself, needlessly wiping down the sparkling counter, cross-checking recipes and shopping lists, and doing all manner of straightening, though, to the untrained eye, her kitchen was already perfection. These many and varied tasks, however, did not prevent her from talking, but hers was little more than mindless chatter: long anecdotes about friends from years past, funny stories overheard at the grocery store, and what little local news there was to share.

Sarah sat, watching Mother Burke moving and talking without end, and wondered how on earth the two would ever manage once Glenn was gone.

The next morning's noisy arrival of Carly changed the house's dynamic for the better. Her years of bartending had honed her skills as an easy and amiable conversationalist; whether the topic was light and breezy, political, or depressing, Carly adeptly knew how to navigate the waters. Tommy's three boys, nearly a year apart each, were barely distinguishable from each other, but it didn't matter. Each was polite, upbeat, and playful, leading to random bursts of laughter, echoing throughout the house.

Sarah and Glenn were still in bed when the troop arrived, and Tommy's orders to the boys rang through loud and clear, his years in the military clearly demonstrated. Glenn glanced to Sarah. She looked at him with such tenderness, he again regretted they'd not had children. Sarah smiled softly at the expression on his face.

"What?" she prodded, her fingers absentmindedly trailing over his naked chest.

"You would've made such a great mother."

She took his hand in hers, kissing his fingertips. "I still can be. You never know."

"Hmm…" he murmured, noncommittal. His eyes drifted to the open window, where the cool breeze brought in the sound of the boys exploring the yard below.

"We don't know what the future holds, hon," she affirmed. "Keep the faith."

Glenn nodded, but knew that his path was set, and no amount of wishing would make it less so. Still, this weekend was all about family and showing gratitude, and Glenn vowed that his illness would not play a starring role. Aside from Sarah, he was determined to tell no one.

"I could not shut her up," Mother Burke was saying when Sarah and Glenn joined the rest in the kitchen. Hugs and greetings were happily exchanged, Mother Burke's monologue continuing throughout. "You know how she was in high school—Betsy Herndon? Well, now she is *Elizabeth*, and you'd think by the way she reacted when I called her Betsy that I'd killed her firstborn. *Lord, give me patience!*' she said to the ceiling. "Well, that *Elizabeth* went on and on, when I ran into her at Walmart about how Glenn was her first love. Like I needed to hear that."

Hearing his name, Glenn tuned in. "Me?"

"Yes, you! Who else am I talking to?" Mother Burke snapped, ignoring the others in the room. "Elizabeth Herndon. Your old girlfriend."

Glenn exchanged looks with Sarah, who'd heard all the stories.

"Oh…" Tommy grinned with a nod. "Even I've heard about her!" he snorted as he stepped outside to supervise his boys.

"She's known far and wide, that one. Well, Elizabeth wouldn't let me go," Mother Burke insisted, "until I promised you'd come for a visit this afternoon."

"What? No—" Glenn managed. "Not the day before Thanksgiving!"

"Oh, come on," joked Sarah. "You'll have fun!"

"You aren't coming?" Glenn pleaded.

Sarah glanced to Carly and her mother-in-law. "I'm off myself, on a quest for a contribution to our feast."

"Oh, don't worry yourself, dear," Mother Burke purred. "There's no need to go to any trouble."

"But I want to, Harriet. Really," Sarah insisted, grabbing the car keys off the counter and giving Glenn a quick peck and wink. "You can take your mom's car."

"But—" Glenn sputtered.

"No hanky-panky, now—you hear?" Sarah sang over her shoulder, bouncing outside.

Glenn blushed, flattered to think Sarah still thought him desirable enough to be the slightest bit jealous.

A few minutes later, he was gone as well, leaving Mother Burke and Carly alone in the kitchen. Tommy had taken his trio to a matinee to give Mother Burke some breathing room, which was just as well with her. His children were sweet and well-behaved, but they were still *boys,* and as such came with all of the usual indelicacies. Her back was sore from picking up the soiled sweat socks and underwear, strewn all over their room.

At the stove, Carly lifted a pot lid, inhaling deeply.

"Cranberry orange relish," her mother noted, with a hint of pride.

"Ooo—my favorite," Carly cooed. "There is something about that dish that just feels like the holidays."

Mother Burke nodded. "Except for the pies, it's my favorite thing on the table."

Carly continued to lift lids and open Tupperware, scoping out the next day's preparations. "Can't we just dive in now?" she pleaded with a laugh.

"I have pumpkin soup for lunch, if you want to heat it up. But you're not getting into anything else without stepping over me!"

Giggling, Carly crossed to her mother, giving her a hug. "Don't worry. I wouldn't dream of interfering with Mother Burke's famous Thanksgiving spread. I know better."

"Well, I don't mean to sound boastful, but I do think this

year will be quite special. And I think we all need it," she added, leaving much unspoken.

"He looks good, though—right? I mean, healthy." Carly looked to her mother for confirmation, but was met with a non-committal smile.

"Glenn will be just fine—don't you worry. He always pulls through," Mother Burke noted. In the fridge, Carly found a bag of baby carrots, which she immediately dug into before offering to her mother, who declined with a shake of her head. "Remember, when he was a kid? That boy was always sick."

Carly looked up at her mother. "Glenbourne, IL."

"What?" Mother Burke looked startled.

"That's what the kids used to say. They would always joke with him: Glenn. Born. Ill."

"That's awful… I never heard that."

"We didn't always tell you *everything*, Mom."

"No…" Mother Burke muttered in agreement, then stopped herself. "But why, though? I mean, why *not* tell me everything? Were you afraid I'd get mad? Judge you?"

"You can be a bit intimidating…"

"Me? Pshaw!"

"Look at Sarah. She walks on eggshells, trying to please you."

"But you've never been scared of me."

Carly let out a belly laugh. "That's because I was a fuck-up. From day one, you knew I was trouble!"

"That's not true."

"You knew I'd shoot straight. I'd call you on your shit, but even if you didn't like what I had to say, you let me say it." Mother Burke could do nothing but nod, as it was completely true. "With Glenn, being sick all the time, you constantly hovered. You'd watch, observe, searching for the slightest cough or a drippy nose. He lived under a microscope."

"But I don't do that with Sarah. I don't *hover*."

"Because you've already judged her," Carly observed. "She threatens you."

"Me? Why should I be—?"

"Sarah and Glenn are perfect together, Mom. They feed

each other, give what the other needs. She kind of took your place."

Mother Burke for once was silent.

"Sarah has tried, Mom. She's made efforts—lots of them— trying to please you. To gain favor. Even now, she's off finding the perfect gift. To make you happy." Carly set aside the bag of carrots, facing her mother head-on. "She wants your blessing. Sarah needs to know that she is part of this family, no matter what happens with Glenn."

Mother Burke looked up, suddenly worried. "Do you know something I don't?"

Rushing over to her mother, Carly clasped her hand. "No! I just meant—*if.*"

"So…" Mother Burke sighed, "I've been a real—uh—?"

"Bitch?" Carly finished, biting her lip, trying hard not to laugh. "Pretty much."

Betsy's parents' house, like most everything else in town, seemed little changed from their school days, Glenn noted. A brighter trim had been chosen, better accentuating its Victorian roots, and the hedges and landscaping had been meticulously overhauled in a distinctly feminine manner.

He heard rushed shuffling noises from upstairs as he rang the bell, and realized he should've called first, but there was something about the way his mom had orchestrated this meeting that made him fight against it. He hadn't seen Betsy since high school, aside from a quick glimpse at their 10-year reunion. His date that night had been in a foul mood, ruining everything, so they hadn't stayed long, but as they were leaving the banquet hall, he saw Betsy emerge from the women's room, smoothing her hair, then taking the hand of Bobby King, who had once been Glenn's best friend.

The door opened and for a brief moment, Glenn thought that Betsy's mother had opened the door. But Mrs. Herndon had been dead for 15 years, at least, and Glenn quickly realized that he was staring into the eyes of his first love.

It wasn't that Betsy looked old, or fat, or ugly. In fact, she looked fit and trim, with just a few stray lines on her face, nagging reminders of the years that had passed. She smiled broadly, showing her teeth before letting out a girlish squeal.

"Why Glenn Burke—I'll be!" She opened the screen, pulling him to her in a tight hug.

"Hey…" came his muffled reply, Glenn's head buried snugly in her shoulder.

"When I saw Mother Burke, I never dreamed you'd actually show up!" She led him into the bright and cheerful living room, which had also had a facelift. "Can I get you something? Iced tea? Coke? Water?"

He shook his head. "I'm fine," he insisted.

"I usually don't drink in the middle of the day, but something about this visit calls for celebration. Wine, maybe?"

"Sure," he granted, deciding it best to be agreeable.

Betsy moved into the kitchen, talking loudly the whole time, and he could hear the chiming of glasses and the popping of a cork, and some other noises he couldn't quite decipher as she rattled on about common friends and schoolmates. Emerging with a bottle of Merlot, she also produced a plate of cheese and crackers.

"Wow," he exclaimed, "this is quite the feast. I realize now that I'd forgotten lunch."

"Well, eat up then!" Betsy chortled. "Don't mind me!"

It was a while before they got around to talking of anything personal, which was alright with Glenn. He wasn't sure if there was an agenda to this encounter, given his mother's prodding insistence that he attend. When the actual topic was revealed, however, it still took him by surprise.

"She told me, you know. About your cancer." Betsy looked at him expectantly, as if it were up to him to respond. But he didn't. He couldn't believe that his mother had told one of Glenbourne's biggest gossips. She should've just sent it to the *Enquirer*. Betsy looked at him purposefully, then asked a question, which seemed to take an eternity. "How *are* you?"

Glenn just stared. "I'm fine…"

"You don't want to talk about it?"

"I'm just—surprised. I mean, we haven't seen each other in years. I figured you wanted to reminisce or talk about Bobby or—I don't know. Not this."

"Does it make you uncomfortable?"

"Betsy—"

"Folks call me Elizabeth now."

"Right. Sorry."

"Your mother told me, Glenn—she shared your news with me—because I am a healer."

"A—?"

Betsy nodded, proudly. "I don't know when it first started. After my parents died, I guess. And I just—I realized that I have a gift. Somehow, in their passing, they gave me a talent, which I can use to make this world better."

Glenn couldn't believe his ears. This was too much. He'd been to the best oncologists in Los Angeles, had every test known to man, tried natural remedies and eaten right, but little Betsy Herndon thought she could cure him. No matter what he'd done, the tests all said the same. He had bone cancer. It wasn't so much a matter of whether he would die, but when. The question itself usually didn't bother him, but returning home to Glenbourne, that question seemed to be all around him.

It hadn't helped that just before leaving, he'd had his blood work done and was anxiously awaiting his results. Dr. Orlan had promised to call before Thanksgiving, but given that the holiday was now less than 24 hours away, it appeared he'd been left hanging.

Crossing, Betsy knelt beside him, taking his hands in hers.

"Betsy—" he stood, dropping her hands. "I really don't—"

"It's okay, Glenn," she assured him, not bothering to correct her name. "You don't believe."

"It's not that. I just—" Glenn looked down at his hands, now empty. "Well, maybe I don't believe. I've tried believing before—"

"Only to have your hopes dashed," Betsy nodded. "I know."

Glenn stared. How much of his illness had his mother shared? Or was Betsy more perceptive then he'd thought?

"I'm not trying to be rude—really. You're sweet and all…"

He let the thought hang, heading for the door before turning back. "You're a healer. That's great. I'm glad for you. But all that chanting and stuff, to me it's just a whole lot of mumbo-jumbo. I'm sorry if that offends you. Really. It may work for you, but that stuff just isn't for me."

He waited for her to protest, but instead she just smiled. "It's okay. I get it. It's not for you. But just as an FYI, I don't do all that chanting. What I do is called touch therapy. And I've already touched you, so—" she smiled pleasantly, letting the thought hang above them.

"What—?" he managed.

Betsy stood, offering a shrug. "The process of healing has already begun."

Sarah combed through every store within thirty miles, but found nothing. Well, in truth, she'd found lots, but nothing that would satisfy Mother Burke. As she finished filling up the tank at Shell, she spotted an old antique store across the street whose paint was peeling, sending rust-colored flakes flurrying out onto the sidewalk. The sign in the store's window read "CLOSED," but as she watched, a weathered hand reached in, turning the sign.

It's part of God's plan, Sarah thought. *This is it.*

Parking the car next to the store, Sarah glanced at the time and realized she didn't have long to find something. *It's hard to believe tomorrow is Thanksgiving.* Where had the time gone? Moving quickly, she stepped inside the store, screen door clanging behind. An old woman with a broken smile greeted her.

"Hi there," Sarah nodded. "I'm so glad you're open."

"Wasn't planning to, with the cooking and what-not, but I got it all done, so figured I may as well, if only for an hour. Thought perhaps there might be a few visitors passing through."

Offering the woman a smile, Sarah began browsing. It was the same collection of discarded kitchen tools, antique tins, and mismatched china she'd seen in every other store. Still, Sarah was convinced she'd find something. *If it is part of God's plan,* she told herself, *I'll find it.*

The saleswoman followed Sarah from room to room, more from boredom than in thinking Sarah a potential thief.

"Visiting relatives?" she inquired, politely.

"Hmm... My mother-in-law. Which is why I need the perfect gift."

"That's sweet," the woman affirmed. "Just remember, dear, it isn't the gift, it's the giving." Offering a wink, she shuffled back to her stool behind the register.

It's true, Sarah thought. *This has caused me far too much worry. It doesn't have to be perfect. It just has to be.*

She sighed, looking about, when her eyes landed on something shimmering near the window. Moving closer, Sarah smiled. It may not have been perfect, but it was darn close.

Mother Burke was finishing the stuffing, readying it to sit overnight, when Glenn returned. Upon hearing his car, she quickly busied herself, uncertain what to expect. Hearing the car door slam loudly, she prepared for the worst. It wasn't the *best* decision, she knew that now, but it had seemed the right one—and still did—though she may pay the price for it.

To her way of thinking, every avenue, each opportunity, needed to be tried and exhausted before giving up. Which was partly why Sarah so bothered her. This "part of God's plan" belief was to Mother Burke merely an excuse for not trying. Why bother doing anything at all, if God knew better and would provide? But, she reasoned, how were they—mere mortals—to know what the Heavenly Father intended? What if, for example, His plan was for Mother Burke to connect Glenn with Betsy? Others might call that interfering, but God might call that intention.

She barely glanced up as Glenn entered, preferring instead to tell him every ingredient she'd put into the stuffing. Not that Glenn cared, as he'd never been interested in cooking, but he knew that this was one of her favorite delaying tactics, and so he just sat, waiting patiently, until she finally drew breath. When she did, Glenn let out a sigh, loud and long, letting her know that like it or not, it was time to talk. She again tried a diversion.

"That Betsy—or Elizabeth, I should say—she is a talker,

huh? When we met at Walmart in the produce aisle she just went on and on and on…"

"Apparently," Glenn eyed her steadily, "she's not the only one."

Mother Burke stopped what she was doing. He was angry, that much was clear. Irritation, she'd expected. Gratitude, she'd hoped for. But the look in his eyes told her she'd made a supreme miscalculation, the damage of which was not yet clear.

"I can't believe you told," he stated, keeping his calm. "Her, of all people…"

"I thought she could help."

"Sure—she can help! Help spread the news…"

With an emphatic shake of her head, Mother Burke interjected. "Not this time. I don't think so."

Staring at his mother, Glenn knew instinctively that she was right. Betsy was a gossip, but only about things that didn't really matter. He had seen, quite clearly, a look in her eyes. No matter what *he* believed, he was certain that Betsy did. She took her healing seriously, so why couldn't he?

He stood, realizing he wasn't up to arguing with his mother, and wasn't entirely certain he should. Instead, he turned without comment, his feet echoing as he moved to the room upstairs.

Thanksgiving morning was awkward all around. The equilibrium within the house had shifted, interrupting its peaceful flow, and no one knew how to reverse it. Mother Burke and Carly launched into full prep mode, readying the turkey and sides, while Tommy and the kids, still in their p.j.s, laid in front of the TV, glued to the parade. Still in bed, Glenn and Sarah lingered in their room, the voices below a low murmur.

Sarah rolled onto her side, propping herself up on her elbow. Glenn had shared with her all the details of what had occurred, but the way in which he'd spoken was odd, subdued. Usually so forthcoming, something about this situation had him unhinged. It was only fitting, perhaps, that it was in mid-conversation last night that Dr. Orlan had called.

From the way Glenn talked, phone held firmly and questions answered methodically, it was unclear to Sarah if he'd received a pass or more bad news. She knew he'd share with her, whatever it was, but prayed nonetheless. *Together, by the grace of God, we can handle anything.*

That morning, Glenn hadn't yet said a word. Instead, he stared directly up at the ceiling. Sarah inched closer, snuggling.

"Do you want to talk?"

Glenn let out a long sigh, his eyes never leaving the ceiling. "This wasn't my room. I had the room right next to Mom's, in case I needed her in the middle of the night. It was small—well, you've seen it—it's now her sewing room. My bed was pushed far against the wall, so I wouldn't be exposed to any draft from the window."

Sarah was quiet, knowing he needed this moment.

"I felt—I don't know—both special and trapped, I guess. I mean, you've never seen folks make more of a fuss over a kid than they did me. And the thing is, there was never all that much wrong with me. I mean, yes, I got sick a lot, but there was never any one disease I was battling or any extended bout of illness. I just happened to pick up a lot of bugs. It got so that even a hangnail would send Mom scurrying for not only clippers but disinfectant... It was nice that she cared—I know how lucky I am—but at the same time, I feel like I never really stood on my own two feet. I was tethered to her—and Carly. I leaned on them, or they propped me up—I'm not sure which—but I feel like I never really was able to claim my life as my own."

As he exhaled, Sarah lightly stroked her fingers over his chest. "They were just trying to help."

"I know, but there were times when I hated them both. I never wanted to feel weak... And yet, if they hadn't been there for me, I would never have survived."

"Those feelings are natural."

"Yeah," he said, rolling onto his side to face her. "But when you never really learn to take hold of your life, you feel subservient. That's one of the reasons I love being with you. You don't coddle. You love me, yes, and you support me, but you also challenge me. We have a nice balance."

"We do."

"I guess what I'm trying to say is that I wish I had more of a balance with Mom. To her, I'll always be that sick little kid, in need of something. I want to live my own life, without my every move being scrutinized."

Sarah simply nodded, placing her hand comfortingly on his chest.

"Whatever ends up happening, I need to feel like I'm in control."

Just before the meal, Sarah approached Mother Burke, wrapped gift in hand. Wiping her hands on her worn apron, Mother Burke smiled broadly. "For me?"

Nodding, Sarah gestured. "Open it."

Mother Burke untied the satin ribbon, tucking it into her pocket for later use, and gently removed the beautiful paper, etched with gold foil leaves.

"So pretty, I hate to ruin it," she grinned. "But I'm gonna!"

Opening the box, she carefully extracted the antique tureen. It was made of exquisite amber-toned carnival glass, which caught the light beautifully. The top formed a chicken, sitting aloft a nest-shaped bowl.

"Oooo—it's lovely," Mother Burke cooed, as Sarah blushed at the rare praise.

"I thought, maybe, for the table, or—"

"I know just the thing," Mother Burke winked, taking the tureen into the kitchen.

Sarah turned to find Glenn watching, offering an impressed "thumbs up."

"Our Father, for these blessings we are about to receive, we thank you," said Mother Burke, head bowed. The family held hands around the table, with Glenn seated beside her. She continued in prayer, offering his hand a gentle squeeze. "This family means so much to me… May you keep us safe, healthy, and happy, Lord. Amen."

"Now let's eat," crowed one of the boys, met by laughter all around.

The food was amazing: a turkey rubbed with butter, garlic, and fresh rosemary, mashed potatoes so creamy they could've been dessert, and a multitude of side dishes. As everyone dove in, assembling their plates, Mother Burke stood abruptly.

"Oops. I almost forgot." She disappeared into the kitchen, then reappeared bearing the amber tureen, filled with her cranberry orange relish. "Looky here, everyone! It's my favorite dish, in my favorite dish!" Sarah ducked her head with a smile as Mother Burke winked.

Glenn reached for the bowl, taking it from his mother. "That looks awesome, Mom!"

"Wait'll you try this," Carly offered, holding out the relish to Sarah. "The mix of flavors, with cinnamon, it is just the thing for the holidays. And the colors—like jewels!"

"Definitely! I missed it last year," Sarah noted with a laugh. "By the time it got to me it was all gone!"

"That's impossible," countered Mother Burke. "I always make too much."

"But you always eat too much, too!" laughed Glenn.

His mother pouted, then chuckled, "You're right. Now pass me the relish!"

The kids had already returned to the TV, this time for football, and the meal was winding down when Carly piped up.

"Okay, it's that time."

Glenn groaned audibly, then yelped as Sarah offered a quick kick to his shin. "Play nice!" she said, sweetly as Carly continued.

"I am grateful for… Tommy, definitely, and the boys."

"Whatever their names are," Glenn quipped.

"And all of you," she continued, shushing Glenn with a wave. "This family—all of you—it's everything. And it's just not the same with you two in California."

His sister had always had a generous spirit, but Glenn, not so much. In fact, he resented being put on the spot with this annual ritual of showing gratitude. Shouldn't it be up to the person to decide if they were indeed feeling grateful? Why only on a specifically-mandated day of the year? Shouldn't showing gratitude be an ongoing element of being human?

He'd felt his mother's eyes on him all morning, silently begging for forgiveness. And although he would eventually acquiesce, Glenn had to admit that there was a part of him that enjoyed seeing the high and mighty Harriet Burke squirm. She seemed to think she knew what was best for everyone, and while that might have actually been the case with him, Glenn still resented her intrusion. He didn't like feeling helpless. Glenn had been born ill, in Glenbourne, IL, but that wouldn't define him. He would show them, through his actions, he had risen above and was his own man, cancer and all.

Still, as they went around the table, he grew more anxious as to what to say. He was grateful for many things, particularly the call last night from Dr. Orlan, but wasn't sure that sharing those details was the best option. After all, he knew better than anyone that a sudden jump in his cell counts, which had been dangerously low for some time, did not necessarily mean that all would be well. The cancer was still there, deep within, hiding, and could again be revealed at any moment. Sharing these latest results might instill false hope, which was the last thing he wanted to do.

Sarah, when it came her turn, had a response ready. "I'm thankful," she said with a smile, "for God and all that He has done in my life. He led me to Glenn, and all of you, who have given me more of a sense of family than I ever had with my own. For that, I'm truly grateful."

All eyes looked to Glenn, who was the last to speak. He took in each expectant face, wondering what on earth he could say that would communicate all he felt and thought inside, the relief, wonder, and endless appreciation for this respite from illness, however temporary. How much their support meant, especially that of his mother, and how rotten he'd felt about how dismissive he'd been about their attempts to help.

With a nervous cough, he gathered his breath, then exhaled with a smile. "I," he said, "am thankful for Betsy."

The next day, Sarah and Glenn packed up, and he took his bag down to the rental car, prepared to return home. As wonderful as it had been to be with family, they were also anxious to return to California, to their new life, new friends, and new opportunities. It may not be their forever home, but the anonymity California offered gave them breathing space from the tangled emotions that stirred here in Glenn's hometown.

As Sarah finally squeezed shut her suitcase, there came a knock at the open door. Mother Burke stood, holding something in her hand. "I'm glad I caught you," she grinned. "I wanted you to have something."

Holding out her hand, she pressed an index card into Sarah's palm.

"I know how much you liked it," she said, then gave Sarah a quick, somewhat awkward hug. Mother Burke started to exit, before turning back with a smile. "You take care of our boy."

Sarah nodded as Mother Burke left, her footsteps echoing as she marched downstairs.

In Sarah's hands, there was a recipe card for Mother Burke's famous Cranberry Orange Relish.

But it was what was on the other side, written in Mother Burke's familiar and steady script, which touched Sarah most:

Please don't share, outside the family.

From the Kitchen of
Harriet Burke

Cranberry Orange Relish

3 oranges	2 apples
1 bag cranberries	1 1/4 cup sugar
1 cup golden raisins	1/2 cup orange juice
1 tsp. cinnamon	1 tbsp. Grand Marnier

Grate 1 tbsp. orange zest. Peel and core apples, chunk. Peel and section oranges, cutting into thirds. Combine all, save oranges and Grand Marnier. Bring to quick boil over medium heat. Simmer until it thickens. Remove from heat and add Grand Marnier and oranges. Put into dish, with plastic wrap on top of mixture, form fitting. Cool in refrigerator.

THE
FOURTH
CHRISTMAS

THE FOURTH CHRISTMAS

ANDREW WOKE, his hand instinctively reaching for the space David usually occupied, only to find it empty. Glancing to the bathroom, he saw no light, and only then remembered David wasn't there. They'd agreed to this separation, their first in four years, assuring each other that it was "for the best." At that moment, however, alone in the dark, Andrew wasn't so certain.

He lay back down, his head hitting the pillow with a sigh, now too keyed up to sleep. *I chose this,* he thought. *I said "yes."*

Nearby, Roxie, their springer spaniel, sputtered, chasing rabbits in her dreams. David had insisted on naming her after the character in *Chicago* who kills her lover and winds up in jail, singing and dancing all the way. Though Andrew couldn't see how that made it an appropriate name for a dog, he'd agreed. Who, after all, could turn down David?

It wasn't that David was impossibly handsome or irresistibly charming. In fact, most would not have found much remarkable about either man, yet Andrew and David saw only beauty in the other. Andrew would spend hours staring at David's moonlit, sleeping frame, memorizing each curve and crevice. When he'd suddenly stumble upon a line that had clearly been there for some time, Andrew would wonder, *Where did that come from? How could I not have noticed?* It was amazing that something he knew so well could continue to surprise him.

They'd met quite literally by accident, four years prior. It was January, and each had been at Anaheim Ice, skating freely

and alone. Andrew was concentrating intently, trying to learn to
skate backward, when David gracefully swept by with a
"whoosh!," startling Andrew and sending him sprawling.

Though David denied it, Andrew continued to believe that it
had not been *fate* that had brought the two together, but David
himself, purposely jolting him. For Andrew knew, when David
reached out his hand, pulling him back up onto his feet, that
David was the one he would spend his life with, and that David
was far too collected for this to have been anything but
deliberate.

And so it was with each step of their relationship—part fate,
part careful calculation. It was not always been easy. Decisions
were made that both would later revisit, but inevitably each
would agree that they'd chosen wisely and chosen well.

Their first year together, Andrew kept pinching himself. It
was hard for him to believe he'd found a man who so fully
complemented him. Aside from David's unfathomable love for
musical theatre, most of their tastes were nicely aligned. Both
enjoyed indie singer-songwriters, hated chain restaurants, loved
thrift store shopping, and ate vegetarian, except for their
occasional late night splurges for burgers at In-and-Out. Still,
Andrew's lack of self-confidence kept him from fully accepting
David's love. At every lull in conversation, he half-expected
David to tell him it was over. But that moment never came.

David attempted to help Andrew see what everyone else saw
at first glance: his gentle sense of humor, his loyalty, his
forthright honesty... These were traits to be cherished, but
Andrew seemed almost unaware. His upbringing had left much
to be desired, and he often wondered how he'd ever managed to
turn out as well as he had. He'd barely known his father, and his
relationship with Natalie... Well, that had been challenging at
best. With his mother, it was a never-ending series of one step
forward, two steps back, but over the years that dance had
grown increasingly tiresome.

From the age of sixteen, he'd tried to educate her, sharing
literature from PFLAG, taking her to support groups for parents
of gay kids, pointing out issues with the scriptures she quoted,

and there were moments it seemed as if actual progress was being made. But each time Andrew would think, *Ah! We are there!*, something else would occur, and Natalie would be just as opposed as ever. This endless ebb and flow, however, gave hope to Andrew of something *more*, but in David's view, the energy spent on her continual push-pull just wasn't worth it.

David's family, on the other hand, was easy for Andrew to embrace. Laughter and warmth abounded in Madeline and Elliot's home. The connection between them was evident and it was clear that they'd showered their children with love, with each becoming assured, well-mannered, considerate adults. Not that they were perfect by any means, but Andrew was surprised to find that their quirks and differences were seen not as flaws, as something to stamp out, but as attributes. It was their varied shapes which worked together, each needing the other to make the family whole.

Spending time with them opened Andrew's eyes to the possibility of living a different kind of existence, and key to that was David's encouragement and support. As their first year together drew to a close, Andrew no longer felt insecure, waiting for the other shoe to drop. Instead, for once, he felt at peace, knowing that all the two shared formed a solid foundation, built on trust.

And so, to celebrate their first Christmas Eve, Andrew and David decided to exchange letters instead of gifts, and read them to each other in the light of the tree. They detailed their love for each other, the value each placed on their commitment, and their shared dreams for the future. It was the first time in their relationship that either used words such as *family, child,* or *forever.* These were vows, though neither called them that, and the promises made would prove far more valuable than any present.

Soon after the holiday, they moved in together, hoping to quickly enact their plans to create the very future they'd envisioned. Year two proved to be about growth, both individually and as a couple. David dove more fully into his job, hoping his efforts would be recognized, while Andrew focused on their home life. He filled out adoption paperwork, child-proofed the house, and interfaced with their social worker. He scheduled their parenting classes and background checks, taking on each hurdle with studied grace and zeal, knowing that being matched with a child would only occur if each of their choices were carefully considered, with more than a pinch of *destiny* thrown into the mix.

It was December when Tyler finally arrived. Fair-skinned and blue-eyed, he was physically different from either adoptive parent, but similar in temperament. Even-keeled and gentle, Tyler brought joy to their home in an altogether surprising way. It seemed almost impossible that a single being could so alter one's very existence, and David and Andrew felt the most fortunate of souls.

But not everyone had seen it that way.

Andrew had just finished placing the Nativity on the foyer table, adjusting the shepherd so that he held his lantern protectively over his herd, when his mother knocked.

Before he could move to greet Natalie in one of their awkward hugs, she stopped him, hand out, barring access. She began to talk, saying things—things he couldn't imagine ever uttering, let alone to his own child. *"You're living a life of sin." "Your actions, your desires—they hurt God." "You and David, you're adults—But a child—an impressionable boy—"*

As she went on, Andrew tried to remain calm, to let all her awfulness slide through him, without trapping any within.

When he was a child, Andrew hadn't given much thought to what *family* meant, but that all changed the day his father left. Suddenly, *family* was all that mattered. He'd remember trips they'd shared and scour each memory in search of something warm to hang onto. What he found, though, were broken shards; sharp and brittle moments pushed aside at the time, of his parents fighting, harsh words, and the occasional slap of a hand.

When he began dating, on every first encounter, he'd assess: *Could this man, one day, be my family?* But every coffee date, dinner, or one-night stand inevitably brought further disappointment, and it wasn't long before Andrew rejected *family* as unobtainable; as something only other people had.

When he came out to Natalie, he thought, *Maybe this will bring us closer, we can be a family, just us two.* But it wasn't to be.

"Think of the child!"

"That's all I do, Mother."

"What kind of affect will this have on him? Do you think he'll ever have friends? A normal life? He'll be subject to ridicule—*you're setting him up for that.* Being witness to your sin will affect him."

"I'll tell you what our nefarious plan is for Tyler. *We're gonna love him.* We're going to shower him with love and give him a fucking amazing childhood. We'll support him, teach him to be kind and smart and respectful, and make sure he's ready one day to take on the world. Yeah, it's a big, bad thing we're doing..." Andrew laughed, unable to stop himself. "You think *we're* going to damage him? Tyler came to us because his birthparents abandoned him. *They left him in a fucking crack house.* But *we're* gonna be the ones to fuck him up. I don't believe this!"

Natalie looked at him, as if for the first time. "It isn't about what you believe, Andrew. It is about what God Himself has instructed."

He eyed her, thinking of all he wanted to say. There were so many points to make, he couldn't possibly address each one. "The God *I* embrace is a loving one," he said quietly. "After all, He made me—and all the other gay people out there. There's no one in this house but good people, trying to do good things. And we're worthy of your respect."

Natalie started to speak, then thought better of it. Instead she turned and walked back to her car, secure in the knowledge that she'd done right by Jesus.

Watching her retreat, Andrew fought every urge to cry out and call her back, to have his dream of *family* restored. Then it occurred to him: *She's never known me, or even cared to know me. She took one characteristic, an adjective as immutable as rain, and stamped that on my being.* All those years, trying to get her to change, he realized, Natalie was doing exactly the same about him.

She'd asked him to choose, between David and Tyler or her, and Andrew had. He chose *family.*

The next year, Andrew and David's third year together, was about change. Learning to live with a child. Learning to live without Natalie. New house, new city, new job for David. Changes in the relationship and changes with their child.

It was November when they noticed. It seemed so impossible, Andrew almost couldn't grasp it... Roxie would bark, Tyler wouldn't notice. His toy train would toot, yet Tyler wouldn't react. His dads would call out, but Tyler wouldn't respond. They took him to specialists, doing every test possible, until the diagnosis was confirmed: Tyler was going deaf.

They'd been informed about the meningitis he'd suffered in foster care, but the extent to which his ears had been damaged still came as a shock.

It seemed patently unfair. To have been given a child—to have fought for their son—in order to give him some measure of well-being, only to discover they couldn't protect him at all.

For the first time since Natalie, Andrew and David found themselves at odds. They debated every option, from hearing aids to implants, trying to find the best path for Tyler. But each question seemed to lead to an argument, and every argument made Andrew fear there was far more at stake than their son's health.

He hated that they fought. Fighting didn't feel like family. Still, a decision had to be made and, as they had so many times before, they approached the matter with careful consideration.

The day in the hospital was endless. An old issue of *Time* and a Snickers bar were all they had to sustain them. A single strand of foil garland hung over the reception desk was the only attempt at seasonal cheer, but the waiting room would've looked better without it.

As they sat, exhausted and anxious, Andrew was reminded of Natalie, and how, as a toddler, he'd had a high fever and she'd rushed him to the emergency room. It had been late then, too, but Natalie stayed, curled up close in his hospital bed. It was one of her few comforting gestures he could remember. Andrew realized he desperately wanted her with him—there at that very moment—to share in his helplessness and despair. He wanted Natalie to comfort him, just as a child, and tell him that everything would be alright.

But she wasn't there and nothing was alright. It was just he and David, hoping they'd made the best choice for Tyler, and praying that their fragile truce would last.

When the long ordeal was finally over, the doctor stepped into the hall and delivered the news. Andrew and David held each other close and cried.

That was one year ago. Tomorrow would be their fourth Christmas, but Andrew was alone. He glanced again to the clock. It wasn't even four yet. He sighed, staring up at the ceiling. He'd always wanted *family*—cohesion—but the absence of Natalie gave proof that mere blood did not a family make.

He came from damaged stock, he knew that now. After all, his father was little more than a name and an address. How had Andrew ever imagined he'd make a good partner for someone? He loved David so much and had thought love alone would be enough. Now, he was beginning to wonder. Love certainly couldn't cure everything.

Being alone made him feel vulnerable, which was the last thing he wanted to be feeling the night before Christmas. *Why had he agreed to this?* He couldn't bear the isolation. He needed David. He needed Tyler.

He needed family.

The bedroom was bright with early morning light as Roxie jumped up and down, excitedly pawing the side of the bed until Andrew again woke. A gentle knock at the door pulled him from his stupor.

"Yes?"

"Wake up, Andrew," sang David's mother Madeline. "It's almost time."

Andrew looked at the alarm clock, which he had forgotten to

set. "Shit!"

"Merry Christmas to you, too."

"Merry Christmas, Madeline! I'll be right down." Andrew jumped out of bed, cracking open the door to let Roxie out, only to find Madeline still standing there.

"I hope one night alone wasn't too hard on you," she offered.

Andrew just smiled.

"It seemed like such a good idea you two had, separate rooms and all," she smiled. "It's like seeing the bride in her gown before the wedding!"

He nodded, for as difficult as the night had been, he'd woken with a new and deeper understanding. Just because his parents had set him off on one path didn't mean he couldn't alter course and forge his own. He could create life as he wanted, unshackled from the past. Indeed, he recognized, he'd ended up doing just that. All he'd ever envisioned for himself was waiting, just down the stairs.

On the fourth Christmas, gifts long since opened and order to the house restored, Andrew stepped into the living room, where all were assembled. Looking around, he took in each face. This diverse bunch had become Andrew's family. *Was it fate that brought them all together, or careful calculation?*

Crossing to the fireplace, Andrew gestured to David, arms open wide. Taking each other's hands and with loved ones watching, Andrew and David exchanged letters, reading aloud the vows each had written to the other on their first Christmas. They shared their commitments of love and lust, trust and faith, compassion and caring, as well as the vow to never again spend another night apart.

And as Andrew and David spoke, softly and tenderly, the glass ornaments on the tree danced with life, Madeline nestled her head on her husband's shoulder, and Roxie, the musical-comedy dog, chased after Tyler as he laughed and giggled, joyously zooming his new fire engine around the room.

HOLES

HOLES

BOBBY GAZED UP AT THE CEILING and again began to count. It didn't matter that he'd counted them before, or that he knew the number of holes by heart—3,016. It also didn't matter that he always counted the same acoustic tile, never changing. The number of holes was something constant; as constant as his mother sitting numbly in her chair, stumbling through another crossword. What mattered most to Bobby was that he knew it. And since he knew it, it could never be taken away.

He sighed, though no one heard it, and thought of Stephen. Blond, handsome, always-with-his-long-hair-in-his-face Stephen. How had everything gone so wrong? Bobby's mind raced over the details of their relationship, sifting through the rubble for clues. The beginning, middle, end.

No one thing stood out as wrong or imminent or foreboding. When Bobby's suspicions were confirmed and it did end, there were the expected rows, and tearful apologies, and scenes in restaurants. But no one could have foreseen the agonizing pain that would come to Bobby. He'd gotten through it, eventually, and now Bobby was alone. Sadly alone.

He filled his time well, though. Going through his Rolodex and renewing friendships. Making dinner plans, and festive theatre outings, and endless gym workouts—anything to stay away from that apartment. The reminders. The memories.

Bobby wasn't completely sure why he missed Stephen. He had always known Stephen would leave. There was no way to hold such perfection for very long. And their relationship hadn't been that great. They bickered. They fought. They made up. And the making up, well, that might have been the reason they stayed together. Stephen and Bobby always had fantastic sex. From that first moment when they'd met at Probe, sweaty and shirtless, sex had never been a problem. In fact, it seemed that the sex was even better after a fight, when it was tinged with anger. So they fought a lot.

There were legitimate reasons for their fighting, however, besides the erotic. Jealousy was a factor. Roving eyes. Then there was the time that Bobby had worn Stephen's favorite Tommy Hilfiger shirt without asking and had spilt Cabernet all over it. There had been hell to pay for that one. And Bobby had relished it. But he was not relishing this.

Again Bobby's eyes drifted toward the ceiling. This had all been years ago. Bobby had had numerous lovers since then, and some had meant much more than Stephen ever had. But no one else had given Bobby the gift Stephen had either.

Anton flounced in at that moment, giving Bobby a peck before launching into an extended monologue about his travails at the cosmetics counter at Bloomie's, where he worked. Bobby's mother, Joan, eventually tired of Anton's high-pitched squeal and left the room, leaving her crossword puzzle behind.

Anton sank into her vacated seat. "I thought she'd never leave," he sighed. "That old bag is gonna get moss on her ass if she don't be careful. She been here all day?" He glanced at Bobby for a reply but got none. "I know she's your mother, sweetheart, but she drives me bonkers. Lord, the two of you are a pair."

As Bobby averted his eyes, Anton picked up Joan's puzzle and proceeded to work on it. "Ooo, she'll have a heart attack when she comes back to find this thing finished!"

His eyes closing, Bobby shut Anton out and thought back again to Stephen. Where was he now? He'd be—let's see, Bobby was 41 so Stephen—just turned 40. If he was even still alive. Bobby had thrown away Stephen's last letter without reading it. He knew what it would say; the same tired mantra shit Stephen had been spouting ever since getting into Twelve-Step. Taking responsibility for his actions, making amends—blah, blah, blah. Could anything Stephen say change anything? Bobby had been through enough and, now that he'd come out the other side, certainly wouldn't take Stephen back. And so he'd tossed the letter into the trash with the other junk mail, full of canned pleas for charity and kindness.

Bobby didn't feel very charitable for that matter, or kind. And why should he? He was the one, after all, stuck here. It wasn't Stephen. Although it should've been.

The doctor came in around seven thirty, whispered something to Joan, and the two stepped outside. Bobby could sense Anton shrug.

The nurse walked in and checked the tubes again. Why did she even bother? Bobby knew that he didn't have long, and as pissed as he was that it was ending, he also knew that there was no chance he'd ever move again. It was too advanced, they'd said. Comes on quickly and then—bam!

Only a week ago, Bobby had been able to form words with his mouth. Only four days ago he'd been able to squeeze his mother's finger to reassure her. Only two days since he'd been able to blink once for "yes," twice for "no."

But that was all gone now. Bobby's eyes still traveled the room, but not at his will anymore. The disease had taken that away, too.

"He doesn't know what's going on at all," the nurse said to Anton.

"He sure looks like he does."

"It's just the morphine... He's probably dreaming. Dreaming wonderful things."

And he was. Bobby's mind floated back to a Fourth of July at Ginger Rogers beach when the guys had built this huge ornate sandcastle to honor the God of Summer. They'd spent all day on it, carefully following Bobby's detailed blueprint. They laughed and carried on, enjoying the sun on their backs and the smell of the fresh sea air. Just as they were finishing, Shirley MacLaine strolled by with a friend, acceding to the boys request to stop and take pictures with the troop and their creation.

The snapshots from that day show Shirley, in all her wigged glory, a mountainous Sleeping Beauty castle, complete with colored flags and drawbridge, and seven beautiful boys in sexy variations of the same Speedo. All with big smiles and gleaming teeth.

The biggest smile of all, however, belonged to Bobby.

But then, that was back in 1982. Back before Stephen. Back before AIDS. Back when Bobby was whole.

THE
OLD RUGGED
CROSS

THE OLD RUGGED CROSS

LOOKING DOWN AT THE LEATHER BIBLE she held in her hands, Cassandra was astounded at the similarity. Both hands and bible were weathered rich, dark bronze, etched with lines and patterns; reminders of their history. She traced the outline of the embossed cross and wondered, exactly, where she'd gone wrong. She'd trusted in the Lord to see her through so many times, it was odd now to feel as if He'd let her down. Los Angeles wasn't what she'd envisioned when she first moved out to be with Reggie. It was a harsh place, where faces smiled but didn't connect. She'd been looking forward to the weather, but even that seemed unforgiving, compared with Jackson.

Back in Alabama, she'd been a domestic, and there was something about the work that suited her. It was honest, leaving her tired but content. That she was to some a cliché didn't much matter. She chose her pace, did her work well, and was paid reasonably. With cleaning, the results of your efforts were immediate and visible. You did the job, felt the ache, saw the outcome. It was simple, really, but satisfying.

In Los Angeles, however, Cassandra was uncertain as to what her job would be, and she'd begun to wonder if moving had been the right decision after all.

It had been Reggie's idea. When he'd first taken his new position, leaving all behind for his dream job of firefighting, Cassandra had been devastated. He was all she had, aside from Jesus, and Reggie's absence made her begin to resent her work, as it kept her tethered to Jackson. They spoke by phone daily, and Reggie would fill her in on all of the amazing people and places he'd met and seen—his optimism was contagious. To Reggie's way of thinking, he'd been dropped smack dab into the land of opportunity, and he was keen that his mother should join him.

For Cassandra, as enticing as the offer had been, it wasn't an immediate "yes." She'd spent her entire life in Jackson, as had her family before her. They had friends, relatives, and support. They had put down roots. But every time she spoke to Reggie, listening to his tales of a far-away kingdom, those roots began to chafe, feeling more like ball and chain than contentment. The more they talked, all she'd once cherished began to seem as if it were her only impediment to happiness.

Reggie painted a picture of a land so desirable, so full of beauty and promise, it never occurred to Cassandra that Los Angeles might be anything but.

She moved shortly before Halloween. Never having traveled very far, the entire plane ride felt like a movie, with Cassandra the only one watching. Everyone around was curiously blasé about their travels, but to Cassandra this was an adventure, each detail of which should be captured.

Arriving at LAX, everything became a blur; people moved so quickly, it seemed inhuman. In the South, there was no reason to hurry unless your house was on fire. Where did all of these folks have to be, and why were they so anxious to get there?

Reggie's friend took her luggage, and the hug her son gave made Cassandra feel that everything would be okay. Driving up La Cienega Boulevard toward Hollywood, Cassandra took in all that passed, searching for some sign of the beauty Reggie had so fervently praised. There were few trees, except some angular palms, which did nothing to shade, and little which soothed the eye. Billboards beckoned, seemingly stacked one atop the other; buildings were crammed together; yards were perfunctory, as if an afterthought. Colors were faded by the sun, which—far from warm and nurturing—felt harsh and unforgiving. A feeling began to settle within, a growing sense that everything surrounding was slowly encroaching upon her personal space, and that feeling could not be shaken.

That same sensation remained when they arrived at Reggie's home, now *their* home. It was functional, which was the best that could be said of it. She faced a white bungalow which may have been charming once, and could be again if only a little effort were put into it. But it sat on a long row of similar houses, just off Sunset Boulevard, making it feel as if it were waiting on death row for demolition. Reggie gave her the master bedroom, which had its own bath, and for that Cassandra was grateful. The minute he was gone, though, she brought out the supplies, scrubbing and polishing every inch of that bath until she was satisfied it was truly clean. While it may have *looked* dingy, she knew better than to complain. *Thank you, sweet Jesus,* she sighed to herself. *I have a roof over my head, with my beautiful son, who is so good to me. Please let me be appreciative of all your gifts, dear Lord,* she prayed, eyeing the rest of the house, in need of cleaning. *And help me find peace.*

By the time Reggie returned the next day, the house was spotless. Reggie noticed immediately how much more pleasant the house was, though he couldn't put his finger on what, exactly, had been changed. Cassandra had put her years of experience to work and not only cleaned, but shifted things *just so* until a better sense of harmony was achieved. She wished she could do the same for her soul, but every nudge off balance sent her scrambling; she did her best to make sense of all she experienced in the world, but the world often didn't offer much in explanations.

When Reggie was ten, he asked to be a fireman for Halloween. Cassandra just stared.

He's his father's son after all, she frowned. *Does he have any idea what I went through?*

Reggie had been only two when his father was killed in a warehouse fire, inadvertently set by vagrants. He was too young to remember any of the details, just the sea of whirling red lights on his mother's face, which looked rather like fireworks. To Reggie, his father was a hero, but Cassandra saw a man who'd taken unnecessary risks.

There were any number of other jobs which would have both suited him and held him from harm's way. Cassandra could've envisioned Carl as a lawyer or scholar or even a preacher. He was commanding, well-spoken, smart—and not just from books. He had an innate sense of what was right and what was wrong, and that moral code was partly why she'd fallen for him so quickly.

As a girl, Cassandra never held much hope for the future. The South was dying, that much was clear, and she had no idea where or if she'd fit in. When Carl came calling, it was as if she'd been blessed by God Himself. She began dreaming of a future together; a life of prosperity and contentment for all three of them. But when that three became two, her dreams narrowed sharply. Each day became simply about getting through unscarred.

Reggie was Cassandra's only remaining source of joy, and she clung to him almost fiercely. And when the day came when he announced he was moving to Los Angeles, Cassandra knew in her heart she'd eventually follow.

Halloween was fast approaching, sending Cassandra into a mild frenzy. She began to fret about treats for the kids and decorations for the house, ignoring Reggie's protests that no kids in Hollywood trick-or-treated. *Surely they must,* she thought. *They're still children, even if they live here.*

She ventured tentatively out onto Sunset, walking past the psychics and ignoring the video stores that sold cheap porn, until she found some suitably spooky decorations and bags of candy at a "99¢ or Less" store. Within no time, Cassandra had the house looking quite festive and sat down to admire her handiwork.

She realized that she missed work. It wasn't that she missed cleaning—though she still found it therapeutic. But she missed the routine; knowing that, at the end of the day, she could feel satisfied with her accomplishments. Here, every day felt the same. She'd get up, eat, bathe, read her Bible, pick up around the house, cook dinner, and wait for Reggie. The problem, though, was that given his work hours she could never quite count on him. Sometimes he'd work nights, and others, days. As a firefighter, he seemed quite content with these shifting times, but she never could get used to them.

Cassandra would sit, eagerly, whatever time he was due, hoping to connect and share, but while Reggie was happy to see her, he was often worn out at the end of a long shift. He'd sit while she heated up his meal, and tell her about what he'd seen, working the fire station, the blazes he'd put out, and the people he'd helped. They were the down-and-outers, more often than not. Sometimes they'd be called to help a homeless derelict causing problems on the street, or a fire alarm might be pulled during a domestic squabble, or a blaze would be set by squatters who'd taken over an abandoned building. And what he saw there—the needs, the desperation, the lack of simple human decency—truly bothered him. But after venting, more often than not, he'd allow himself one tumbler of scotch, then excuse himself, leaving Cassandra alone.

She was alone that Halloween. Shopping, she'd seen countless furry costumes, and wondered why on earth someone would choose to wear one of those in Los Angeles. It was hot, incredibly so, even in October, and the mere thought of wearing something so suffocating made her feel short of breath.

Creating a spot for herself on the porch to best greet the children, she made a pitcher of strong lemonade, filled to the top with ice, which she put on a small table. Cassandra sat, staring up at the sun, which had not yet set, and wondered what she would do with herself.

"The world is yours!" Reggie had exclaimed, but Cassandra doubted even he'd believed it. This was Hollywood, after all. Her options were few, given her career history. No one cared about her many years of cleaning. True, she could've found work again as a domestic, but the whole point of this adventure had been about *change*. Why settle for what was comfortable? Plus, as Reggie had not-quite-jokingly pointed out, she wasn't getting any younger. As if she needed to be reminded.

As she sat, she scanned her newspaper, folded to the

employment section. Admin. Clerk. Driver. Exotic Dancer. Retail. None felt quite right. At this point, Cassandra wasn't looking for money. While she didn't have a lot, she had managed to save, but she had saved for a life in Jackson, which was substantially less expensive than a life in Los Angeles. Still, she wanted something that would not only bring income, but that would help justify her existence. Not that the job need be grand. It simply had to be one that used her skills, challenged her, made her feel useful... Sitting on a stool in a store wasn't it.

Cassandra looked down at the highlighter in her hand, realizing she hadn't highlighted a thing. Glancing up again, she saw that the sun had just set and readied herself for Trick-or-Treaters.

They came, though only a handful, and most seemed to know no English, aside from "Please" or "Thank you." Still, they were much nicer than the older boys who stopped, not even in costume, demanding candy. She'd given it, despite their attitudes, only to be questioned whether she had any candy that was "bigger." Cassandra held out her bowl to prove to them that everything was the same size, but they viciously reached in, scooping up as much as they could, before running down the street, leaving stray pieces and laughter in their wake.

Cassandra watched until they were out of sight, then moved inside and shut off the porch light. But instead of feeling angry at being abused, she felt sorry for them. Where were their parents? Had they been taught to behave that way or was that survival-at-any-cost learned on the streets?

That's what life without love looks like, she thought.

"You can't just sit here all day, Mama. It ain't good for you."

"And fighting fires *is?*" she parried, having had this conversation before.

Reggie sighed, crossing behind her and placing his hands on her shoulders to give them a squeeze. "I've told you before, it's my passion. If you felt passionate about sitting around the house, I'd let you do just that. But you sit, waiting for me all day, with no other connections. You need to get out, meet people..."

"You don't want me around?" Cassandra sniffed, not very convincingly.

"You know that's not true. Stop being dramatic."

"Me? *Dramatic?* Well, I never—"

Reggie laughed, "Ah, yes you are! Think I don't notice all your hems and haws? The eye rolls?" He opened his eyes wide in exaggeration, making Cassandra finally laugh.

"Okay, maybe a little..." she admitted.

"My point is, Mama, I love that you're here. I love your company, and that you take care of me, and your cooking—"

"Yeah, I knew you wouldn't forget that—"

"But you need a life outside of me. When we were in Jackson, you saw the family, went to church, had friends..."

"I have friends here."

"Watching me and the boys play poker now and then don't count."

Cassandra frowned.

"All I'm saying," he continued, "is think about it. What do you like? What do you enjoy? As big as this city is, there's gotta be people you'd like or things you'd enjoy doing. You just need to find your passion."

While Cassandra saw his point, what Reggie couldn't see was that she *was* passionate about two things: him and God. She thought Reggie hung the moon. And God, well—she was having issues with Him. She'd trusted that once settled, He would speak to her and give her some guidance. She prayed and read the Bible daily, waiting for Him to speak, but he'd been very quiet lately.

In Jackson, God walked with her daily. She'd talk to him in her head, and sometimes out loud, while doing her chores. Each day she'd end with "Thank you, sweet Jesus, for letting me be of service and for helping me do a job well done."

It crossed Cassandra's mind that perhaps she'd somehow displeased God. She'd felt certain that He'd wanted her to move to Los Angeles, but made she'd been mistaken. Maybe He was punishing her for being here, in what her Aunt Cissy called the "land of heathens." True, maybe Los Angeles wasn't an *ideal* place to be, but if Reggie was there, it couldn't be all bad.

It was still hot at Thanksgiving. Reggie kept telling his mother to get out and enjoy the sunshine, but Cassandra felt most comfortable indoors. It wasn't only temperature, but something else she couldn't quite put her finger on. One day, it hit her: Hollywood wasn't supposed to be there.

The town had been built on a desert, which no amount of tinsel could quite disguise. It was a hot, primitive landscape, which eventually wore down its inhabitants. The goal here was to get rich and get out, but far too many fell short of their dreams of glory. They failed, like countless before, and ended up fleeing back to their hometowns, or parking themselves in the Valley, where they served younger up-and-comers at bars, restaurants, gas stations, and shops. It was a bleak view, Cassandra realized, made all the more bleak by how few even seemed to care.

As the heat stretched out into December, Cassandra longed for the green of Jackson. For the ample stretches of grass, rolling out, as far as her eye could see. She'd never thought of Jackson as cool, given the humidity, but there was something about it, a freshness most often felt in early morning, which rarely happened here.

It was a Wednesday, a week before Christmas, when she first learned about Reggie. She'd been expecting him and had dinner set, when the knock on the door interrupted her preparations. Through the screen door she saw the men in uniform and hadn't even had to ask. She just knew, standing there, that her baby boy was gone.

Just as with Carl, she'd always known this work was dangerous, but—even so—Cassandra had long believed the Lord would see Reggie through. While she'd never believed God played favorites, she'd been such a firm believer, devout, Cassandra had allowed herself to assume that nothing bad could ever happen again. But it had.

They told her the details, but she made them repeat them twice to be sure she got it.

It wasn't a fire? No. Not a fire.

There was a man, lying on the steamy pavement, so parched and broken someone thought him dead. Reggie's crew, responding to an errant alarm just down the street, had immediately come to his aid.

Reggie bent over the man, checking for signs of life, when the man thrust up, again and again, knife in hand, gouging repeatedly. Not even realizing he'd been hurt, Reggie attempted to subdue the man, helping to calm him, when one of his men noticed the blood. Brushing them aside, he ordered *"Get that guy some help,"* but it was all too clear to his crew that it was Reggie who truly needed help.

Cassandra couldn't remember saying anything afterward. She just remembered seeing the back of the men's uniforms as they returned to their car.

She called Aunt Cissy immediately, only to be greeted by her answering machine. Cassandra spoke, but couldn't remember what she'd said. Had she even mentioned that Reggie was dead? She called Cousin Judith next, but got a busy signal. She picked up the phone again, only to realize she didn't have anyone else to call.

She sank into a chair, receiver in hand, and cradled it to her chest. Her breathing came heavy, soon joined by deep, anguished sobs. *My baby, dear Lord. My baby boy! What have I done to you? Oh, Lord, what have I done?*

Her tears continued as she rocked herself, phone in hand, speaking to it as if it were her Reggie.

In the months after his death, Cassandra couldn't break herself from her habits. She'd wake, bathe, eat, pick up the house, read, cook. Nothing meaningful. It seemed, in a way, that she was keeping her routine, never varying, in the hope that one day she'd turn and Reggie would be sitting in the chair opposite.

The only part of her routine she neglected was her leather-bound Bible with its embossed cross. Her daily readings stopped, so angry was she with God. The Bible first sat beside her bed, but even the sight of it would rile Cassandra so that she banished it to a drawer, piling other books on top, as if to suffocate it.

Damn you, Cassandra thought, raising her eyes to the heavens. *Why have you forsaken me?* She waited for a moment, but got no reply. *Well,* she sighed, *if the line was good enough for Jesus, it's good enough for me.*

Cassandra was about to head into the kitchen when she stopped herself. When had she begun to joke about Jesus? What had happened to her?

Reggie was right, she thought, *I need a passion, now that both of mine are gone.*

She got calls from Jackson now and then, urging her to return. *"We're your family now, Cassandra. We always have been." "What's holding you there?" "You need to start planning for your future."*

But that was the problem. When she thought about the future, Jackson didn't feel like *it.* How could that be, though, when L.A. didn't feel much like home either?

She thought of other places she might like to visit and other towns in which she might live, but they were all *somewhere else.* Los Angeles, like it or not, was where Reggie was and would now always be.

"You the woman of the house?"

Cassandra just stared. She'd been asked that question a million times back in Jackson, and always had an answer at the ready: *"Mrs. Whoever can't come to the door right now. May I leave word as to who is calling?"* More often than not, the salesperson would simply nod and bid her good day, but this was different. This was her house now. She could do as she pleased, she realized. *What would please me most,* she thought, *would be to slam the door in this young man's face,* and she started to do just that.

"Please ma'am! Give me a moment. Just a few minutes of your time."

Cassandra held the door ajar, peering into the man's dark eyes. His rich ebony skin and confident smile reminded her of Reggie. She frowned. "What are you selling?"

"Me?" the young man's brow furrowed. "I'm not selling anything. I'm collecting donations for kids with cancer."

"So you want money?" Cassandra demanded, not so much a question as fact. She would not allow herself to be manipulated by a scripted plea for charity.

"Actually, we'll take anything. Clothes, furniture, appliances... Everything donated gets a tax deductible receipt, and we have a truck picking up items on Thursday. If you'd like to help, just place any items in this yellow bag." He held up the plastic bag in offering, but Cassandra scowled.

"You want *my help?* My son *died*, young man, just a few months ago. Nobody helped *me*. You don't see me with my hand out."

The young man looked down, respectfully, until he was sure Cassandra was done. Then, very quietly, he raised his eyes to hers. "What was his name?"

Cassandra felt herself gripped at the neck, so much so that her hand instinctively reached to it. *Who was she anymore?* She'd been awful to this boy and he gave only kindness in return. His generosity threw her so off-kilter that Cassandra was clueless how to respond.

Breaking her eyes from his, she closed the door, locking access to the outside world.

As Memorial Day approached, the news tributes to fallen veterans began to take their toll. These men and women died, yes, but so had her son. All were in the line of duty. All were honorable. Yet these few, who'd gone to war, were singled out as somehow more worthy of praise, of remembrance, than those who sought to keep peace. Where were the holidays for firefighters? For the police? Shouldn't all public servants be valued?

It's bullshit, she thought. *All of it.* She'd sought meaning, some explanation from God on how she'd had failed him, and been met with silence.

On TV, the President was laying a wreath at a soldier's grave, prompting Cassandra out of her chair with a harrumph. *They only do that on holidays*, she thought, *when there is a camera pointed at them. They don't live every day, as I do, like it's Memorial Day.*

Cassandra realized she had to get out of the house. That

feeling she'd had on her very first day in the city, of everything caving in, was happening again, only this time it was the house itself. She felt like the walls were moving ever-so-slowly, inching toward her. But Cassandra resolved not to be helpless, to not be scared. Instead, she grabbed her keys and headed outside.

The heat had again returned to the city. *How odd, to have only a few months respite,* she thought as she walked, without destination. She would never get used to city living. Wandering, all she saw were weeds, beer bottles, and forgotten grocery carts. There were forgotten people too, on the edges of her sightline, and she was reminded again of Reggie. His desire to help had led him to this city, to his job, and to his death.

Still, she reckoned, he'd probably have wanted it that way. He'd rather have died being of service than to have lived a wasted life. Which is what she'd been living lately. She had retreated from the world, taking the easy route, instead of being an active participant.

Looking up some time later, she realized that she had followed Fountain Avenue all the way to where it dead-ended at Bronson. She was literally and figuratively at a cross in the road. If she turned left, up to Sunset, or right, down to Santa Monica, she'd be walking in places crowded with the homeless, graffiti, and trash. Or she could reverse, returning more safely back down Fountain toward home. It should have been an easy decision, but Cassandra took a moment nonetheless. *Which way, Lord? Which way???* Not getting an answer, she shrugged before heading north, only to stop herself. There was nothing but urban blight ahead. Cassandra turned, prepared to head back the way she'd come.

"Hey!" someone yelled, catching her attention, but Cassandra saw no one. She took another step, only to hear, "Where you think you're goin'?"

Gazing about, Cassandra spotted an old woman across the street, her shopping cart overflowing with possessions. With her ill-fitting clothes, weathered skin, and tangled hair, Cassandra assumed her to be homeless, especially when she spotted a stuffed bird pinned in her hair. Cassandra smiled and nodded politely before resuming her walk back toward Fountain.

"Think you can run?" the woman shouted. "You can't! You can't run from Jesus!"

Cassandra stopped dead in her tracks.

That was what she'd been doing ever since Reggie had died, running from the Lord. She blamed Him, questioning His wisdom. She'd asked the Lord for explanation or understanding, only to be ignored.

But the thought occurred to her: what if He hadn't been silent? What if He'd actually been speaking this entire time, only through other people? For all Cassandra knew, He could be speaking through this homeless woman... What if the old crazy lady wasn't as crazy as she seemed?

Turning, she found the woman still eyeing her. Checking the street, Cassandra crossed, taking stock as she approached of the woman's toothy grin. She waited for more from the woman, but was greeted by silence and a smile. Cassandra looked down at her feet, then again to the woman.

"Are—are you Jesus?"

"What—?" the woman erupted into cackles. "Ooo! You think old Angie is Jesus? Ha! Oh Lordy—you crazier than me!"

"I don't know who you are," Cassandra offered, "but you sure called me out... Saying I was running from Jesus. I figured you might as well be Him."

Angie hooted and cawed, "Oh, honey—if I was Him, you best believe I'd be making a whole lotta changes to this place," she gestured around her. "Make life a bit nicer."

Cassandra stared. If this woman wasn't Jesus, she sure was saying all the right things. Jesus had helped the poor, shown compassion, healed the sick, and even raised the dead. What had Cassandra done lately, aside from feeling sorry for herself?

She nodded to the woman's shopping cart. "You okay?"

"Nothing a fifth of gin won't cure," the woman grinned, showing some missing teeth, before reaching into the cart and pulling out a puppy. "Look at this little thing. Peed itself, all over my sweater." She held it close to her chest, stroking the puppy's back. "It was my fault. Should've let him down when it was whimpering."

Giving the puppy a kiss, the woman then returned it to the

cart, which she began pushing down the street. Cassandra watched as the woman left, shaking her head the whole way, repeating, "Thought I was Jesus! Thought *I* was Jesus…"

She stood, until the woman could no longer be seen, then wondered which way she'd been headed. *Toward Sunset,* she remembered. *How appropriate. I'm on a pathway leading up to a brilliant sunset.*

Cassandra started walking up toward the boulevard. She was still unsure where she was headed, exactly, but thanks to Angie she was certain that the path would include doing the work Reggie had begun, helping others. Service was a concept to which she could relate. She wanted to again feel a burst of pride, some sense of accomplishment, that she was doing something worthwhile. As Reggie had said, she needed a *passion.* With him, it had never been a question of whether to help, it was a question of *how.* Now, it seemed, Cassandra too felt the pull.

She couldn't help smiling as she walked, taking note of how something as simple as making a decision, of taking one step, could turn around her entire way of thinking.

The old rugged cross had never let her down. The Lord had been there for her, time and again. It was time Cassandra finally returned the favor.

HEARTS

HEARTS

"I HATE BEING JEWISH." Even as the words passed her lips, Karyn could feel the eyes of her mother, Bea, fire up, despite having been dead five years.

"No, you don't," Kevin insisted, proving himself, yet again, a reliable voice of reason.

"The problem is," she continued, blindly, "I don't believe much in anything. Judaism, Christianity, Buddhism... It all seems like a bunch of hooey. And Atheism makes perfect sense, but—I'm sorry—it's just not uplifting enough."

"That's true," Kevin nodded. "But whether you believe in something greater or not, or all the dogma that goes along with religion, you'll always be Jewish. It's in your DNA, so best make peace with it."

"You're right, Kev. I know that," Karyn hated to admit. "I mean, I've lightened my hair, straightened my nose, worked on my diction—I'm still the same girl."

"For the life of me, I don't know why you do it. I mean, look in the mirror. You're beautiful, just as you are. You need to embrace your inner Rachel Berry. Just be *Jew.*"

"This, from the gay boy who keeps track of his caloric intake in a journal...?"

"In my world, that isn't about wanting to be something you're not. It's about good health."

"And your bicep tattoo, despite your fear of needles? And those ridiculous shorts? Are those about health, too?"

Kevin brushed aside her accusations, well aware of how Karyn liked to turn the tables, as well as how little time they had before the lunch bell rang. "I, for one, am not subverting myself," he sniped. "I am gay, simply fitting in with my tribe. You, however, are trying to disassociate yourself from yours. Not that you ever can."

He had a point, which irritated Karyn.

"Besides," he continued, "look at all of the great old Woody Allen movies. Diane Keaton: neurotic, sexy, *and* Jewish."

Karyn laughed. "Neurotic, yes. Sexy, yes. Jewish, no. More the ultimate WASP. Which is what I'm trying to be, without that *P.*"

"Regardless. My point: you are both sexy and neurotic, and you need to embrace that."

"Me? Neurotic?"

"Oh, don't give me that—you know you are. Being neurotic has nothing to do with being Jewish and everything to do with being raised by Bea and Herschel."

"So I'm neurotic, *not* from being Jewish, but by being raised by Jews? Nice."

Kevin pushed back from the table. "I give up."

"You always do."

"There is no winning with you, Karyn. You won't allow it."

He was right, of course. Karyn continually felt the need to win. Actually, not so much *win*, as *dominate*. She chalked up this particular trait to being Jewish as well. There was something about coming from an entire community that had been persecuted for generations that made her want to fight back. She'd been taught to be assertive, to get what she wanted without apology, but now that she wanted to rid herself of her heritage, suddenly found others angered. Karyn recognized that she was breaking the mold, but failed to see how her personal desires could negatively impact another. What did it matter?

Still, in the hope of salvaging the moment with Kevin, Karyn changed tack.

"So-o-o," she asked, stretching out the word, "who are you taking to the dance? Anyone?"

"Aw, I don't know," Kevin muttered. "There's no way in hell Josh will go. That would be too much of a political statement."

"But it's our last high school dance before prom," she pushed. "And it's Valentine's! You two lovebirds should be together."

"That's exactly what I said, but you know Josh. His closet door is made of granite; there's no chiseling that thing open."

"It's a shame, really," Karyn offered. "I mean, who cares if his father is a right-wing, bigoted pastor, and if simply acknowledging the truth would put them both on the evening news. *So?* There are worse things..."

Kevin laughed, knowing it to be true. Josh had compelling reasons for the choices he made, which had been fine, up until now. To Kevin, though, he couldn't quite identify with all of the angst Josh had undergone. It was a simple choice, Kevin noted, between living authentically or living a lie. Why was that so hard for Josh to understand?

For Kevin, coming out had been a breeze. The only difference between *before* and *after* was the enormous weight he'd felt lift off his chest. He was able to inhale, freely and fully, without constriction. Yes, his family had made it easy for him, telling him they'd known since his first few years of life. He realized that coming out wasn't necessarily as easy for everyone, but to Kevin, it was clear: love was worth the risk.

Karyn knew better than to push it with Kevin, though she'd always been firm: Josh would never change, as long as his father was alive. It was a losing proposition, with disappointment the only thing left at the end of the road. Kevin deserved better. He was a steadfast friend, putting up with all Karyn threw at him. She knew he needed someone who valued him wholly.

Karyn eyed him curiously.

"What?"

"I'll be your date," she offered with a shrug.

"What about Dougie? Or have you already tired of him?"

His questions were met by a slow and steady exhale. "Oh, he's such a child."

"He's 23. Five years older than us—and he's hot!"

"Hot, yes. Smart, no."

"That's true."

"I need to be challenged. Stimulated. And by that I mean,

stimulated by more than just his dick."

Kevin pulled out his phone, flipping to his photos. "Oh my God, the first time I saw Josh's dick—"

"I don't need to see it, Kevin. You know I support you, but I'd rather you leave out the screenshot."

"But you just talked about Tommy—"

"It wasn't like I showed you our sex tape."

"*You* have a sex tape?"

"Just one more way to break the Jewish stereotype."

Kevin sat back, eyeing her. "Why are you so unhappy, being Jewish?"

"Oh, come on, Kev—Jews always get the short end of the stick. Folks think we're cheap, untrustworthy complainers."

"And what are you doing right now?"

"I'm not *complaining*. You don't hear 'Oy vey' coming out of my mouth, do you? Ever?"

"No. But that doesn't mean you don't complain."

"What I'm trying to say is that other folks have it better. You Christians get all the best holidays, ones you can count on. Ours bounce all over the place, like grease on a hot griddle. And, for the most part, ours are all rooted in pain, repentance, and suffering. Fasting *does not* a fun experience make."

"So, Easter, with Jesus hanging bloody, dying on the cross… Good times?"

"But you don't celebrate that. The resurrection you've morphed into cute little bunnies and baby chicks. I mean, it's hard to argue with pastel colors."

"I see your point," Kevin admitted as the bell rang, signaling their return to class. "When I was young, I thought I'd rather be Jewish—you know—for the eight days of presents. But then I was over at Sammy's after Hanukkah and added up all he got. My haul totally blew his out of the water. So I stuck with J.C."

"We'd better move," Karyn noted, seeing that they were among the last at lunch. Quickly gathering their backpacks, they began to part ways. "Think about the dance," she called out.

"I'll go," Kevin nodded enthusiastically. "But only if you'll be my Valentine!"

For as long as Kevin could remember, Karyn had been unhappy with herself. It bothered him to think that she could not see what he saw. Her mode seemed permanently set to Google street view, focusing only on each perceived flaw, even if that flaw had been removed long ago. Kevin, however, believed that *satellite* was the only way to view yourself, to realize that you are part of a larger community. *We are but one piece of the puzzle,* he believed, *and we need each unique piece to make us all whole.*

He began to consider just how amazing Karyn was and all that her friendship had brought him. He was a better person now, and that could be directly traced back to her. She had enriched him, challenged him, doing for him exactly what she wanted her boyfriend Dougie to do for her. What she couldn't seem to see was that Kevin was already playing that same role for her. She'd be so much happier, if only she could get her loving from Dougie and her learning from Kevin.

There must be a way, he reasoned, vowing to find it.

The dance was the Friday before Valentine's, which was in fact the following Thursday. While this didn't make any sense, it fit better into the school's sports calendar, which dictated everything else. Adding to this buffoonery, the student council had engaged a band instead of a DJ, which meant the band would sing songs no one knew and the dance would suck. Given all of this, Kevin decided the way to make the most of the night was to plan a special surprise for Karyn beforehand, and went to work immediately.

It would be tricky, to balance it just right, so that she didn't take it as romantic or ill-considered. But if he could deliver, it just might help Karyn see how fierce she truly was.

The night came quickly, and Karyn was prompt. Kevin opened the front door to find her looking phenomenal. For the occasion, she'd selected an unexpected buttercup yellow dress, which complimented her spray tan nicely. She wore her blonde hair up, though not severely, allowing her face to be gently showcased. She'd clearly used the Crest White Strips he'd given her for her birthday, leading to teeth that sparkled. In a word, she was gorgeous.

"Wow!" he managed. "You look—"

"Amazing," she finished. "Yes, I do," Karyn smiled with a laugh. "You're always telling me to value myself, so—*here I am!*"

He ushered her into the living rom.

"So, where are we going? Red Lobster? Applebee's?"

"Nah! Would I let you eat there for Valentine's?"

"You mean week-before-Valentine's, *dumb-shit school.*"

"Exactly. Well, I've decided on a much more exclusive dining option for tonight's meal."

"You're making me nervous, Kevin."

With that, he gestured grandly toward the kitchen. "Voilà!"

"I got dressed up to eat in your breakfast nook?"

"No, silly! We're eating in the dining room."

"Seriously—you're scaring me!"

"Come on," he laughed. "When have I ever steered you wrong?"

"When we drove all the way out to Palmdale, when we were supposed to be going to San Diego?"

He grinned, shaking his head, acknowledging she was right. "Just go in."

Though her eyes squinted warily, Karyn did as she was told.

Entering, she stopped, taking in the table impeccably set with china, glowing candles, and the hearts taped to every bare surface.

"Wow. Definitely a step up from Red Lobster."

"Ya think?" Kevin laughed.

Karyn looked around. "So where is everyone?"

"My folks are having Date Night, and I gave Jerry twenty bucks to go to the movies."

"I hope you're not planning on putting the moves on me..."

"Sorry to disappoint, Princess, but Kevie don't play that way!" he offered her his arm, guiding her to a chair. "Sit. Your waiter will be with you momentarily."

Taking her seat, she placed the napkin onto her lap, marveling at the exquisite table. In between the glittering votives, candy hearts were strewn about, their messages, such as "You're cute," "Be mine," and "Hot stuff," facing toward her.

She picked one up and ate it. As she did, Kevin walked back in, donned in an apron and wearing a fake mustache.

"Bonsoir, mademoiselle. Voulez-vous boire quelque chose?"

"Um, is that some kind of champagne? You know I'm underage."

"I was asking if you'd like something to drink. Water? Soda? Fruit juice?"

"Sparkling water with a slice of lemon, please."

"Coming right up," he smiled, gliding back to the kitchen.

Karyn couldn't believe he'd done all this. The time and effort he'd put into creating this dinner, just for her, was enough to make her want to cry. He was one of the few, it seemed, who *got* her, in all her eccentricities. He never asked that she change or demanded she be anything other than who she was, and his unwavering belief in her was somewhat hard to fathom.

Again, Kevin appeared, bearing drinks on a tray, which he quickly set down before scurrying back to the kitchen and returning with their meals. Karyn stared at the steaming plate before her.

"Wow, Kevin, I'm in awe. You made all this?"

"Yes I did, if 'making' includes heating. I bought the coq au vin and scalloped potatoes at Costco, but I did make the salad. I mean, I opened the bag and tossed it."

"Still," Karyn marveled. "You did all this for me?"

"Well, I was going to make it all from scratch, but when I realized I'd have homework and stuff too, I figured this was a safer option. But, yes, it's for you."

"I'm totally floored. I don't know what to say."

"Don't say anything... Just eat."

Finally full, Karyn sat back, still marveling at it all. "So, does Josh know you went to all this trouble for me?"

"Well, about that... We broke up."

"What?!? When?"

"Monday."

"And you didn't *say* anything?"

"It isn't that big a deal."

"That big a—? He was your first love! Where are the tears?

The gnashing of teeth? The pulling out pages of hymnals?"

"I'm fine. Really. It was my call and I just—I realized that I can't live life afraid. I can't worry about what the neighbors think, or my family. Josh lives for others, but I need to be my own person... I don't see how we can create a better world if we're not first honest about who we are."

She looked up at him. "Are you still speaking of Josh, or me?"

"Both, I guess."

"You think I don't live honestly?"

"I think you are honest—brutally, at times, in counting all of your faults. But I think you're dishonest too, in not counting everything else."

"What are you talking about? You think I don't like myself?"

He let her comment sit for a moment. "Are you done eating?"

As she nodded, he stood. "Take my hand." Again, she did as told.

Guiding her, Kevin walked her over to one of the walls, papered with hearts. "Read one."

She looked at them, brow furrowing, then selected one, pulling it from the wall. "Um, 'Karyn saw me crying, came over, and put her arm around me.'"

"That was when Josh dumped me—the first time. Read another."

He randomly pulled one down, handing it to her.

"This one says, 'Karyn made the whole class laugh when she told the moose joke.' Oh my God, that is right! I'd forgotten about that."

"Keep reading. I'll be right back."

She took another, and another, and still another, reading each notation about her moments, large and small. They captured a whole range of incidents and emotions. Some were funny, some sad, but all were *Karyn*, in all her varied shades.

When he came back into the room, carrying a gift-wrapped box, Kevin saw that she was crying.

"What's the matter...? I thought you'd like it."

It took Karyn a moment to respond. "I'm not sure why you did this, exactly, but thank you."

He crossed to her, giving her a hug. "I wanted you to see yourself as I do, and others do. You focus so much on the negative, on whatever you think makes you less than—like your heritage—but that isn't what people see. They aren't focused on your pimples—"

"Oh my God—where?"

"—not that you have any, or the little scuff on your shoes, or how your hair looks. People are looking at the big picture—at least, the people who matter are—and you need to embrace that. Be *Karyn,* in all your complexity. Own it. Own that sexiness. Own that neurotic craziness. Own your smart, caring self."

"You mean, 'Just be *Jew?*'"

"We are *not* getting into that again. Stop pigeon-holing yourself. There is so much more to you than any one thing." He handed her the large, wrapped gift. "Here."

"What is it?"

"Duh. Open it."

Karyn slowly untied the velvet ribbon, removing the floral print paper. "It's so pretty." As she opened the lid, Karyn smiled, pulling out a black men's hat.

"Do you know what it is? From *Annie Hall?*"

"It's perfect, Kevin," Karyn sighed in awe, slipping the hat onto her head. "Just like she wore. Wherever did you find it?"

"eBay, silly. You can find anything there, from corn to porn."

She hugged him closely, "I wish you were straight... You really are my best friend."

He smiled, placing a sweet kiss on her forehead. "Okay, it's time to go, but before we do, one more thing."

"Not more presents!"

"Just remember this, my dear. You are *amazing.*" He walked over to the table, coming back with a candy heart. "Sexy, yes. Funny, yes. Neurotic, yes. Etcetera, ad infinitum, and on and on. You are you. Look at the big picture, and always remember this..." He placed the candy heart into her hand, which read, *You Rock.*

Karyn smiled, pulling him in for a hug and a quick peck on the cheek. Blushing, he started to pull away. "Own the praise, Kevin. If you're telling me to, you need to own it as well."

He nodded with a grin before running up to his room to grab his jacket.

Crossing to the hallway mirror, Karyn turned, admiring her new hat. Pulling it off, she reached up and let her hair down, giving it a shake. As Kevin returned, she placed the hat back onto her head, pleased with how it flattered her.

"You look terrific," he noted.

"I know," Karyn laughed. As her laugh softened into a smile, Karyn looked him in the eye with a sigh. "Thank you. Truly. I've never felt more beautiful."

"Good," he said, pulling her to him in a hug. "Now you see what the rest of us do."

She blushed, grinning.

"So, this is *it*," Kevin said, expectantly. "The moment. Our last stupid dance of high school before prom. You ready?"

As she nodded, Kevin opened the door, ushering her out. She pulled him close as they walked arm in arm to his car, allowing her head to rest gently on his shoulder.

MOTHER'S
DAY

MOTHER'S DAY

EVEN THOUGH DARKNESS HAD FALLEN, Evelyn could see each line reflected in the mirror clear as day, as if a map had been imprinted on her face. The road traveled was decidedly marked, its angular ridges and deep crevices a stark reminder of each decision she'd ever made. She'd long known her choices would make her unpopular, but had felt, in God's eyes at least, she'd done alright. Until today.

Evelyn had waited patiently for a call, but none came. No flowers had been delivered, either, nor gifts, leading her to dread each interaction with others in the home. Lucy Baker had gone on endlessly, chattering about how amazing her girls were and how generous they'd been. Florence what's-her-face, usually pleasant but bland, was boastfully showing off the drawings of her granddaughters, as if the crude scribbles were worthy of a museum. Even Charlotte Hibbs, the meanest woman on the floor, had received a large bouquet of roses, delivered by FTD.

But Evelyn received nothing.

In total, her boys had proven disappointing, even as children. Her eldest, Bobby, who had always hated his nickname and insisted on *Robert,* was a constant complainer, bucking the system—and Evelyn—at every turn. He'd left town right after graduation, with only the odd note giving any indication as to where he was or what he was doing. Her replies seeking more information inevitably went unreturned. Evelyn had no idea who was to blame or where he had gone wrong, but was certain that drugs were involved.

George, on the other hand, had been a relatively easy child, if a bit dim. Grades were continually an issue, and Evelyn had worked diligently to keep him on track. He'd married Olivia right out of high school, despite Evelyn's repeated warnings, and had moved all the way to Orlando, as if miles alone were all that were needed between him and his mother. He worked at Disney World, which seemed a very stupid place of employment for a 40-year-old. But he and Olivia seemed quite happy, though Evelyn hadn't a clue as to why. At first, they'd kept in touch, calling and writing, but the efforts slowly became more and more infrequent, and Evelyn blamed Olivia.

It had been eight years since the two had Claudia, and six since Christopher, but Evelyn had yet to meet either. George had offered to fly her out, but a flight meant going through Dallas, and that airport had always terrified her, so Evelyn stayed put. George seemed upset, taking it personally, as he always did. He pointed out other means of transportation, noting that it was easier and less expensive for her, an individual, to make the trek, than in uprooting all four of them. To Evelyn, though, he was just lazy and self-centered. Weren't children to show respect to their parents? Hadn't Evelyn and Frank provided for them, as they should? Though Evelyn had no proof, it was clear to her that Olivia wore the pants in that family. She could easily picture Olivia in the background, pulling strings, planting seeds, goading him on, encouraging the divide between mother and son to grow ever wider.

Still, as much trouble as Bobby and George had been, it had been Thom who was Evelyn's greatest disappointment, which started in the womb. Having had two boys already, Evelyn felt certain her third would be a girl. Frank would continually rub her belly, cooing to it, whispering sweet nothings to his baby girl like a fool. Friends and family alike pointed to signs and omens, assuring her that she was indeed having a daughter, so much so that Evelyn had begun planning as such. She'd poured through the Sears catalog, picking out new furnishing, and compiled a wish list for her shower, filled with dainty and frilly things. Finding out they'd all been wrong was the first in an endless string of disappointments with Thom, each one worse than the last.

Frank had a soft spot for Thom, which to Evelyn seemed a flaw. There was something suspect in the way Frank coddled Thom, clearly bonding with him more than their other children, which irked Evelyn endlessly. Must the baby in the family always be the favorite? Frank held Thom in a special place in his heart, apart from the rest, and Evelyn could not see how any good could come from that. It seemed a weakness, and reminded her of the time she'd shown up unexpectedly at the law firm and seen Frank perched familiarly on the corner of his secretary's desk, laughing and leg swinging. She felt certain nothing untoward had occurred, but still felt jealous at having been left out of their fun. And it seemed the same between Frank and Thom. Their bond was so strong, so complete, there was little room for anyone else.

She'd long been taught to spare the rod, spoil the child, and Frank's gentleness toward the boys seemed to hold that concept in contempt. He continually prodded her to show more kindness and understanding, which only served to bring him down a notch. Years of disagreements separated the two even further.

When they'd first met, Evelyn had held her tongue as she'd been taught. She praised Frank at every opportunity, at her mother's urging. "The way to a man's heart," Gladys had preached, "is through his ego." It had been helpful advice, too, as evidenced by their speedy engagement. Friends had assumed that she'd been careless and become pregnant, but Gladys had advised to reel Frank in quickly, before he saw what lie beneath and change his mind.

He regretted marrying, she knew that now. He'd made that clear in his final days, urging her to seek help, *therapy,* so that she didn't make her sons' lives any worse than she'd made his. He recounted each perceived slight and every unkind word. He wanted her to change, as if he had been the perfect parent. Frank had been quite nasty, indeed, which Evelyn blamed on his medications.

Evelyn saw no point in sugar-coating things. Why pretend? She believed in acting authentically, even if that meant being disliked. She wasn't a fool and wouldn't be taken as one, ever.

She lived by God's rules, not man's. It was He who created the ten commandments. It was His word she listened to each Sunday, and read about. She had to answer to Him, in the end, not Frank. And not Bobby, George, or Thom either. Evelyn would only answer to God.

From the time she was nine, Evelyn went to mass daily, rain or shine, and often alone. Her father worked, and it seemed her mother often couldn't be bothered. She'd go occasionally, if Evelyn prodded enough, but begrudgingly. It frustrated Evelyn to no end: How could you not want to experience the beatific vision of God Himself? What was more important than that?

Her parents tried to reason with her, to get her to see that there was more to life than church, but Evelyn didn't see it that way. God was everything. She needed nothing more.

Even Father Demitri reached out, which Evelyn found shocking. He said she was missing the point of faith. That faith meant believing so fervently, so deeply in one's soul, that you could let go of rigidity and find a sense of inner peace. He preached of kindness and charity, and the importance of opening up one's heart to the world. He gave her the whole song and dance, but Evelyn knew better. Belief was something you had to hold onto and feed. The world would go to great lengths to destroy faith, challenging it, so faith needed to be protected as one would riches, with walls.

She began to build a fortress around her heart, allowing no one in, to keep it safe. God would reward her, she knew. It would be difficult, to be unpopular, but honesty and piety would be rewarded when she met her Maker.

It had been 10 years now since Thom had shared his news. Ten years since she had seen him last. She'd been right about his being soft. She'd known something was wrong with him, and she'd been right.

Frank had been adamant: *be kind, show some compassion, open your heart...* But Evelyn would have none of it. It was against God's will; against His word. Thom was going to hell—that much was clear.

Thom cried and pleaded, whining that this was who he was, and it was just as God had intended. But Evelyn knew God far better than Thom, and shook her head in scorn. That such a mistake as Thom could have come from her own body horrified her. *I've done something wrong,* she thought. *Somewhere, I made God mad.*

That had been the end, for her, of not only Thom, but Frank. He couldn't believe she could act so heartlessly, he'd said. He moved out soon after, saying he couldn't put up with her cruelty any longer, and that he should have done it long ago.

But who was called when he fell ill? Evelyn.

She'd known that he'd need her one day, and he had. She visited daily, putting up with his endless pleas for a sign of kindness, as if her very being there was not.

He received daily phone calls from both Bobby and George, and daily visits from Thom, propelling Evelyn out of the room each time. She wouldn't give in, no matter who pleaded. There were moments, even, when she wished Thom had never been born. She knew such thoughts weren't remotely Christian, but she had them just the same. God was testing her with Thom, that much was clear, but she would not be broken.

After Frank died, Evelyn continued on, resuming her routine: wake, eat, mass; wake, eat, mass... The retirement home had been Olivia's idea, she felt sure. George was the one who suggested it, but Evelyn could smell the scent behind it. It was for the best, he'd said. With both boys living miles away, Evelyn needed someone to watch out for her.

She'd protested at first, but relented in the end. She attempted to get closer to Bobby and George, but both kept their distance. They were all she had now, besides God, but again they let her down.

Life may have disappointed her, but God never did. She knew it, felt it, with every fiber of her being. In choosing God, she had made the right choice and he would reward her for it.

Still, given the day's events, a Mother's Day spent in silence, she couldn't help but wonder... She prayed, that night, for a sign. Some signal from God that her faith, her devotion, placing her every trust in Him had been worth it. That she'd not lived her life in vain. *Send me,* she prayed, *a sign.*

The tingling began in her arm, but soon became a shooting pain, racing across her chest tightly as if she were being squeezed. She gulped, gasping for air, as the band across her body wound tighter, punishing her. Her eyes whirled about, searching for someone—anyone—to help, but she was alone.

Her eyelids fluttered, and the fluorescent lights above turned into blinding white, piercing through her. God was calling, or someone was, talking loudly to get her attention. Just before passing out, she heard the voice clearly. It was Thom, her Thom, urgently calling out her name.

FATHER'S DAY

FATHER'S DAY

AS BETH INHALED, STEADYING HER COURAGE,
Angelica reached over, offering her hand a reassuring squeeze.

"You okay?"

Beth nodded, "I'll be fine."

"You don't have to, you know. You owe her nothing."

"But you're wrong, hon," Beth smiled wryly, shrugging. "I owe her everything."

Engine still running, Angelica unbuckled, turning and leaning toward Beth. Reaching over, she ran her fingers lightly through Beth's hair, trailing down, her palm gently cupping Beth's cheek. "I know she's family, but so are we."

Beth leaned in, offering a soft kiss in return. "I feel so fortunate. Meeting you that day... Even with the rain, you totally drenched—I'd never seen anyone more beautiful. Having you in my life has made me a better person." She reached down to Angelica's growing bump. "And you! I can't wait to meet you, either!" she laughed, offering the bump a rub. "I wish I could go with you..."

"It's just a checkup. You can miss one, you know."

"Yeah..." Exhaling, Beth let out a sigh. "I promise I won't miss another."

Angelica grinned. "How did I get so lucky?"

"Luck had nothing to do with it," Beth replied, stepping from the car before leaning back in. "It was your sweet ass that did it."

Entering the unappealing and antiseptic room, which looked a bit like a clean Motel 6, Beth smiled at Carlos, who was plumping her mother's pillow. "Good morning!"

"If you say so," he muttered. "She's quiet now, at least."

"Fun, for all of us!" Beth laughed. "Boy, Carlos, you're a better man than me."

He looked over, lips pursed and eyes arched knowingly, before they both burst out in laughter.

Her mother's eyes flickered, recognizing the sound, then settled swiftly back into dreamland.

"How much did you give her?"

"Normal dose, though I would've liked to have given more."

"Difficult morning?"

"You could say that, I guess. But adding an adjective like *extremely* would help."

"God bless you, Carlos. You are a saint."

"Me?" he laughed. "I get paid. You though, you put up with her since you was born. The saint crown goes to you!"

With a wink, Carlos was off to check on his other patients, leaving Beth with a parting smile. The long, low sigh she let escape her lips filled the room. She hadn't known that simply walking through a door every day could be so hard. Beth took in her mother's sleeping frame, so small and brittle. She looked so at peace, her mouth almost a smile, that for a fleeting moment Beth wished her mother would die, right then and there, so that Beth could hold onto her smile, instead of the face that so often haunted her dreams.

She couldn't remember her mother ever smiling, though surely she had. Instead, Beth's earliest memory occurred when she was three. She'd snuck quietly into her mother's room, though it had been expressly forbidden, but the beautiful sprays shimmering in their cut-glass bottles and the array of cosmetics, all in varying shades of red, could not be ignored.

Alone, the afternoon sun bathing the room a brilliant orange, Beth began to explore, pulling out drawers and trying on clothes, particularly those that felt soft against her skin. She applied potions, endlessly putting on and taking off, her discarded tissues forming a white and red mountain, until she found just the right look that said *Beth*.

It was her unexpected mother's murderous look, though, which told Beth all she needed to know. She'd done wrong, clearly, and not just in a *bad girl* kind of way. What she'd done had been distasteful somehow, abhorrent even, and only served to instill in her mother a deep-seated drive to annihilate any joy Beth might discover in life. Even now, as an adult, Beth was unclear exactly what she'd done to have prompted such fury, as she'd heard similar tales of exploration from others that ended far differently. But with Beth and her mother, the dividing line had been made plain that very day.

What began as a mere gulf stretched continually wider, the sea between an incessant, tempestuous churn. Throughout elementary school, Beth couldn't, or wouldn't, conform to rules firmly set, which led to regular meetings between parents and staff. Her mother would cajole and berate, prodding Beth to tow the line, but her father looked at her differently, with clear and focused eyes. He understood but couldn't, or wouldn't, intervene in her mother's wrath. Perhaps he was afraid of his wife or, better yet, knew that voicing the truth would only put Beth further in harm's way.

Removed from the angry voices and squinted eyes, Beth would sit by herself at her desk in her room, door closed and pen in hand, and write the *th* in her name over and over again. She filled binder after binder with an endless string of *thththth*'s. There was something about the way the letters fit together, complimenting each other, which gave her comfort. That *th* was distinctly *Beth*.

As months turned into years, Beth learned that the best path to peace lie in success and conformity. She tried obeying and fitting in, studying every night and turning herself into the model student. With each report card, her mother's eyes would spark approvingly, forgetting herself, if only momentarily. And so the awards and accolades began to pile up, making Beth think that finally all might be right. But it wasn't.

She was 14 when she began cutting herself. It had given her, if not exactly pleasure, a sense that Beth was indeed *there*. There were times it seemed as if Beth were scraping, cutting down to the bone, to better reveal her true self. Other moments, it felt more like, in piercing her skin, she was ensuring she could still *feel*. Her years of subterfuge led her to question just who she herself was, so deeply had Beth suppressed her most honest desires.

Her mother sighed, smacking her lips. Beth raised her eyes from her novel, *Being There*.

"I didn't get that movie," her mother grunted.

"The book is better."

"It usually is," her mom coughed, leading to a string of hacking coughs. Beth set down the book, reaching over to refill her mother's water. Inserting a straw, she moved to the bed, holding it to her mother's lips. Her mother's eyes squinted sharply.

It's killing her, Beth thought, *to be here, reliant on me.*

"I love that line though, in the movie…" Beth offered, "where Jack Warden says 'life is a state of mind.'"

"You would," her mother grunted disapprovingly, smacking her lips for more water. "Always in your head."

Beth thought of a million comebacks, most of which were vengeful. Instead, she gave her mother another sip before returning the cup to the bed tray.

"Do you want me to turn on the TV?"

"God, no. All those awful Bravo shows, with the women who scream at each other."

"There are other channels, Mom." Beth smiled. "And I'll gladly turn on any one of them you'd like—except Fox News."

Her mother sighed, closing her eyes. "Then there's nothing worth watching."

Beth couldn't tell if her mother was being serious or not, but decided that she was. Debating her next move, she glanced to the wall clock, which seemed of another era altogether.

Angelica is likely to be in with the doctor by now. How does she do it? she wondered. *Putting up with me, pregnancy, my crazy family. It is she who gets the saint crown, Carlos, not me.*

As if hearing his name, Carlos appeared in the doorway. "Everything okay?"

"Lovely," Beth smiled. Her mother uttered a grunt that made clear she was not in agreement. "Have my brothers visited?"

Carlos shook his head, "Just you, baby girl!"

"Father Pitori?"

Again, Carlos' head shook a "no." He smiled with a wave, heading back to his tasks. "You're all she's got." His footsteps echoed, receding as he journeyed down the hall.

How sad, to have purposely charted a course to a deserted island. I won't live like that, Beth vowed.

The low hum of her mother's breathing told Beth that she'd again fallen asleep. She was grateful for the quiet. Conversation that should have been mundane, about books, or television, or even soap, seemed difficult to maneuver, let alone talks about "life."

Beth picked up her book, then realized she'd just finished it. *I should've brought another. Next time, I'll be prepared. A bag of books, some gift for Carlos, and a pitchfork... Or body armor. Maybe a nice blouse made of chain mail.*

A knock at the door prompted both Beth and her mother awake. Angelica stood there, beaming, hands on belly. Beth launched from her seat, embracing Angelica, as her mother averted her eyes.

"How'd it go?"

"Swimmingly," she smiled, returning Beth's hug. "All signs point to a healthy baby."

From the bed came a cough, then a muttered, "Does she have to be here?"

Beth spun about immediately, then checked her anger as quickly as she could. "Angelica is my family. If you want me here, she is as well."

"You think I care if you're here?" came the reply. "I couldn't care less."

Eyes darting, to avoid the tears she knew were coming, Beth forced a smile. "Fine."

Walking briskly to recover her purse and book, she attempted to remain calm, unsuccessfully. "But, just to be clear, Mom, that is the problem. Your 'not caring' is exactly why you're here. Why you're alone. Why your kids and grandkids don't visit. Why you have no friends. People are scared to be in the same room with you. Even your own priest won't visit," she laughed. "You created this situation, this life, by remaining bitter and angry and insensitive. Despite all of our efforts, your anger is the very reason you're here. A life lived in anger can't help but cause—this..." Beth gestured to the room around her. "Not to mention everything else."

She glanced to Angelica, whose jaw had dropped open. "Angelica is my family. She gives me support, encouragement— yes, and love—the way that families are supposed to. I'm not sure why she loves me, as screwed up as I am, thanks in no small part to you. But she does. Angelica's made me see that I'm of value—that I mean something. My whole life, you saw nothing good, but Angelica sees only gold. And all that stuff you didn't do, all the things you should've done, I'm going to make sure that our child has that. We will make sure that he—or she— feels loved. Supported. Regardless of who they are or who they choose to be. We will love them."

With that, Beth turned, heading resolutely toward the door.

"Thom!"

The room went silent, save for the low rattling of the air conditioning vent.

Eyes locked with Angelica, Beth debated how to best respond. Angelica tried to communicate, through her eyes, that Beth had done well enough without her help. Beth reached forward, cupping Angelica's belly, which held her very own child. She'd created life, a new life, and was determined to create a better world for it than the one she'd known.

Turning slowly toward the bed, her voice was as even as she could manage. "It's Beth now, Mother. You know that. It has been for some time."

Evelyn stared silently, lips pursed. She took in Beth, staring directly into her eyes, and was startled to realize she wasn't looking at her son at all, but a strong, confident woman. Evelyn then looked to Angelica, anxiously twisting her hair around her fingers, and followed the curve of her rounded belly, contemplating *what that meant*. That child was a part of them— all of them. She wondered what Father Pitori would say, and realized she didn't care anymore. She'd been so concerned with what she imagined God thought that she'd never much considered how she herself felt.

Evelyn had pushed Frank away, and George and Bobby— *Robert*. Not to mention Olivia and the grandchildren she'd never even met.

Beth was right. She had created this. Unknowingly or not, this life had been entirely her creation.

Evelyn sighed, taking note of the room around her, with its stark white walls and muted furnishings... She'd always thought of heaven as being bathed in white. Others might have looked upon the room as harsh and sterile. A blank space, a prison, for a life misled. But Evelyn took in all the white and blankness, suddenly seeing in it a vast canvas of possibilities. She had a choice, she realized, and it was entirely up to her: give up all she'd held close—change—or continue to follow the road she'd set for herself so many years ago. While she wasn't entirely certain she even could change, or would end up being happy, she knew her previous path had led only to heartache.

She turned, looking again into the eyes of her daughter. "Will you visit again, Beth?"

Beth's eyes watered, but she immediately forced back her tears. It was hard to know with her mother. Was this an olive branch or yet another false start?

Angelica gave no clue as to her thoughts. This was Beth's decision, after all, which Angelica would respect.

And so, as she had many times that day, Beth sighed, gathering courage, and again faced Evelyn. "Yes, mom. I will."

A DORIS DAY
CHRISTMAS

A DORIS DAY CHRISTMAS

JEFFREY AWOKE WITH A START and immediately ran to the window. The night he'd dreamt of was finally here, making sleep difficult at best. It was still dark and he knew there would be hell to pay if he was discovered up. Still, he peered out into the yard, pitch black, with no movement of any kind. Even the trees, full with the weight of newly fallen snow, were strangely silent. Jeffrey ran to his bedside table and grabbed his flashlight. Bringing it to the window, he sent a bright sword slicing into the yard's deepest shadows, hoping to uncover... what? A fat old man in a red suit? Rudolph? A six-foot tall present, bulging at the sides? But as Jeffrey looked, he saw nothing.

It was stupid really, Jeffrey told himself. He was much too old for this kind of nonsense. Shining the beam onto the sleeping mound that was his brother, Jeffrey frowned, climbing back in bed. The arms of the clock glowed in the darkened room. It was not even midnight. And that was too early for Santa anyway, wasn't it?

With a sigh, Jeffrey rolled onto his side and tried to shut his eyes. He'd need every ounce of strength to get through the next day if Santa hadn't come through for him. It was a tall order that Jeffrey had put in, but wasn't that the old man's job—making dreams come true?

It had been two years since his father died, and in the time following, Jeffrey watched as his family shifted, morphing into something he didn't quite like. Seemingly afraid to be on her own, his mother, Maggie, remarried to a loathsome bore named Dirk, a plumber, whose only social grace was that he kept his mouth shut when he chewed. Jeffrey's little brother Bryan retreated from life—literally. He now lived in a large cardboard box, and wouldn't come out for anything. They'd tried bribes, pleas, and threats, but Bryan remained hidden, firmly entrenched in his flammable cocoon.

Bryan was given his meals in the box, took his nap in the box—even brought it to bed with him, though it remained *next to* the bed; Bryan safely ensconced beneath the covers. Occasionally they would catch a glimpse of Bryan's pale arm as it would creep toward a plate of cookies, but that was about it. Jeffrey was unsure exactly what Bryan looked like anymore, so hungrily did the little fist pound down its cookies. He could've been three hundred pounds and they would never have known.

While Bryan's change was understandable, to some extent, and could be explained away as a youthful quirk, there was a change in Jeffrey's mother, too, which was far more puzzling, though not as pronounced. Anyone who hadn't seen her for a while would have immediately noticed the transformation, but to those around her, the changes had appeared slowly, subtly. First, she dyed her hair blonde and fashioned it into a popular bob. Next, she started wearing brightly colored party dresses at every occasion, however inappropriate. Further, her mannerisms became almost unbearably cheerful and upbeat. On and on went the metamorphosis until Jeffrey finally realized what was happening: Little Maggie Clements from Omaha was doing everything within her power to turn herself into Doris Day. Not only did she see every movie that Doris made, including the stinkers, but she even started paraphrasing lines and bits from these movies. In fact, just yesterday at breakfast, when Jeffrey said he wanted only one piece of toast, she crowed, *"With Six You Get Eggroll!"*

As strange as these changes were, Jeffrey could deal with them, because they were happening to members of his family. His new stepfather, however, was another matter altogether. A burly hunk of a man, Dirk enjoyed his wife's new look, presuming it was all for his benefit, and took pride in escorting her to bowling, just to show her off. Unfortunately, those happy moments were rare. Exceedingly rare.

Immediately after marrying Maggie, Dirk pulled Jeffrey aside and said, "Look, kid"—Jeffrey was certain Dirk didn't know his actual name—"I ain't your old man, and I don't wanna be. He's dead and buried, six feet under, and the sooner you get used to it, the better." Jeffrey was six at the time. "And don't go putting your old man on a pedestal, neither," Dirk snarled. "He was a mean, rotten—"

Maggie interjected, *"Love Me or Leave Me*—just don't curse!"

"All I was gonna say is, kid, you'd better watch your P's and Q's, or you're gonna be just like him."

Welcome to the family.

That first Christmas with Dirk was the absolute worst. When Jeffrey's father was alive, the boys would wake up early, running in to see the tree. The rule was that they could open their stockings but had to wait for the presents until everyone was up and accounted for. Dirk, however, liked to sleep in. "It's the one friggin' day I get to sleep and I'm takin' it. Anyone who comes near me before ten gets a sock in the eye." And so, Jeffrey and his brother in the box sat by the tree for two hours, fuming, not touching a thing, until Dirk lumbered down and had his coffee.

After presents, the boys were used to playing with their new toys until mom was ready for their annual Christmas brunch—a feast for the senses, made entirely from scratch. But Dirk liked football, and declared that the family eat leftovers in front of the TV, and stay there until all three games were over. "I don't want you kids runnin' about, yelling your stinkin' heads off. I want peace and quiet and—quiet."

Jeffrey had thought that Christmas couldn't possibly get any worse, only to learn that Dirk had planned, as the piece de resistance for their holiday celebration, a "fun-filled" family night at Bowl-a-Rama.

For these and other reasons, Jeffrey hated Dirk. He longed for the day he'd see a policeman sadly walk to their door, dripping plunger in hand. As Jeffrey played with his toys, he'd come up with countless new and exciting ways to kill Dirk off. He tried bows and arrows, Chinese water torture, the rack, skyscraper fire, bullet between the eyes, cattle stampede, and spontaneous combustion, just to name a few. Though Jeffrey's G.I. Joe didn't seem to enjoy these games, Jeffrey was set and determined to finally rid the world of Dirk Diamond, making his house a home once more.

At last, a plan materialized. He'd come upon the idea on Thanksgiving night. *Miracle on 34th Street* was on television and, as Jeffrey watched little Natalie Wood walk with wonder into the new house and spot Santa's cane, he realized he'd struck gold. That was it! Of course! Why waste time coming up with a plan when there was already a simple solution to his misery? Santa would make his Christmas dream of a normal family come true.

It was two weeks later, a Tuesday afternoon, when Jeffrey got his big break. Packing his brother and accompanying box into the car, Jeffrey's mother turned to him and said, "Santa's at Gilman's. Want to come?" Jeffrey almost scoffed, feeling too old to sit on Santa's lap, then remembered his plan.

As quickly as he could, he was piled into the back seat, strapping himself in beside the box. For once, Jeffrey did not pound on Bryan's box, nor threaten to write rude things over the Bekins label. He had more important things on his mind. Much more important.

Once at Gilman's, as the new Doris led her two children toward the line of anxious faces, Jeffrey scoped out the competition. It was obviously a train and Mystery Date kind of crowd, though the red-headed kid in front looked like someone who'd typed up his entire list—all eight pages of it.

With a sigh, Jeffrey tried to relax and arrange in his head the words that would make his fantasy a reality. He shuffled around words and phrases, changed the emphasis of the "please" and "thank you's," working himself into such a state that he was nervous to even spit the words out.

Finally, it was Jeffrey's turn. Shyly, he walked toward the old plump gentleman, patiently waiting, and was promptly scooped onto Santa's lap with the help of the antsy elves. After getting his name and good/bad status, Santa leaned down and asked the all-important question that Jeffrey had been waiting to answer. "And what do you want for Christmas, Jeffrey?"

With a bashful smile, Jeffrey leaned up to the old man's ear and whispered his request. Santa sat back for a moment, perplexed, before managing a smile and a pat on the head. "I hope your Christmas is a merry one, Jeffrey. You deserve it."

As Jeffrey ran back to his mother and brother in the box, Santa looked at Maggie with an enticing smile. "I don't believe I've talked to you yet," he said, taping his fingers together. Jeffrey's mother turned four shades of red.

"Oh Santa, I'm not–"

"Come on up, little girl, and tell Santa what *you* want for Christmas."

After first checking to make sure no one she knew was watching, Maggie plunked onto Santa's lap with a giggle, smoothing out her aqua blue party dress.

"I can tell you've been a good girl this year. And such fine sons, too. But I want to know what you want for Christmas."

Maggie thought for a minute, then offered with a silly laugh, "Um, just a *Touch of Mink*."

"Is that all? How about–?" Santa pulled Jeffrey's mother close and whispered.

Jeffrey leaned forward, hoping to hear, but all was lost in the din of the holiday crowd. Just as Maggie turned towards Jeffrey, eyes wide and mouth open, a tug from the box at his elbow sent his attention elsewhere.

The ensuing days flew by, filled with fun and frolic, as Jeffrey was able to put his worries aside, confident that Santa would take care of *everything*.

Finally, the big day arrived.

Jeffrey woke up with a shout and shook Bryan's bed. "Wake up! Wake up! It's Christmas!"

The lump on the bed moved slightly, Bryan's box still next to it, in its place, which meant one part of his Christmas wish hadn't come true. And as he raced down the hall, he heard the familiar, "Shut up, knucklehead! I'm tryin' to sleep!," and realized the second part hadn't happened, either. And when, a short time later, his mother appeared at the top of the stairs in her brightly colored dress, Jeffrey knew that Santa had utterly failed him.

As the presents were unwrapped in their usual fashion, Jeffrey felt betrayed, but went through the motions, acting as if he was thrilled with the new G.I. Joes.

"I noticed your old ones were a bit worn," Maggie said with a smile. "You can do anything you want with these, but *Please Don't Eat the Daisies!*"

Jeffrey tried to smile at his mother's little joke, as she'd been happy with the picture of Doris Day he'd painted for her, but his heart wasn't in it.

Finally, as the rest of the family settled into an afternoon of football and TV trays, Jeffrey pleaded sick and returned to his room upstairs.

At the window, Jeffrey gazed out on the other boys and girls, playing in the fresh snow with their new toys. They had each gotten what they wanted. Why hadn't he?

He hadn't heard the door open, but Jeffrey knew from the floral scent that his mother was at his side.

She reached down and stroked his hair. "What're you thinking about?"

"Nothing," Jeffrey lied.

"You want some food? Something to drink?"

"No. I'm fine. Really."

Maggie perched next to him, pulling Jeffrey close. "It was a nice Christmas, huh?"

"Yeah. Thanks for the toys. They're great. I can't believe Dirk got me a bowling ball…"

"Did Santa bring you what you wanted?"

"Just about."

Eyeing him fondly, Maggie pulled Jeffrey even closer and sighed. "Did I ever tell you about the cat that barked?"

Jeffrey shook his head no.

"It was a long time ago, when I was a girl. It was the

strangest thing you ever did see. A neighbor's cat, actually—not ours. And it barked. Not a meow like all the other cats, but a very distinct 'Ruff!'"

"Like a Dachshund?" Jeffrey asked.

"More like a German Shepherd. Deep and sort of scary. In fact, my friends and I would hear that frightening bark, and we'd cross to the other side of the street just to be safe."

"You were scared of a cat?" Jeffrey asked, incredulously.

"Oh yes! And the other cats were, too. None of them would go near him, he was so different."

"So what happened?"

"One day," Maggie sighed, "I was walking home from school late—I'd been held over by Miss White for talking—and all my friends had already left. I was all by myself. And as I came around the corner of my house, I heard it. The bark. And it was very, very near. 'Ruff, ruff. Ruff, ruff.' It got closer and closer and—"

"Did you run?"

"I thought about it. I may have even turned around in the other direction. But then it hit me: it was just a cat with a bark. Why should I be afraid of it just because it was different? And so I walked right up to that old barking cat and, ever so nicely, patted it right on the head. From that day on, he and I were the best of friends."

"You're talking about Dirk, aren't you?" Jeffrey asked, suspiciously.

"Why would you think that?" Maggie looked surprised.

"He's loud, and scary, with kind of a bark."

"Oh honey," Maggie laughed, planting a kiss on Jeffrey's forehead. "I can see why you think that, but he's really not such a bad guy. He acts tough, but Dirk is just like any of your friends playing out there in the street."

"No, he's not."

"Each one of those kids has a bark. In fact, every person in the world has one. Something that makes us different. Some of us wear them on the outside, and others… we wear them on the inside. But everyone gets one. Just a little something to make us stand out."

Jeffrey cried, "But why do we have to stand out *so much?* Why can't we just be normal, like everybody else?"

"Honey, that cat could've hidden his bark by not barking. But he'd still have it. He may look the same as all the other cats, but whatever he does, he'll always be different. So he'd better learn to love that bark."

"Are you saying I have to love Dirk? Because I don't want to."

"Honey, you don't have to do anything you don't want. Just remember, though, when you're getting tired of Bryan being in the box, or angry at Dirk, or embarrassed by me, everyone has a little something about them that makes them special. You may not like their bark. Or appreciate it. You may even be afraid of it. But whatever you do, don't ask them to stop barking. Because that barking is what keeps us alive."

After his mother left, Jeffrey watched the boys and girls playing below and tried to figure out what the bark of each was, exactly, and what was his. He contemplated this for a while, then, yawning, he stretched out on his bed for a snooze. And as he did, he had the most wonderful dreams.

They were different dreams than usual. A mixture of old and new, familiar and fantastical. Everything, however, was warm and comforting, blending into a swirl of images that felt like family.

As he slept, the sun slowly setting over the house, Jeffrey dreamt of Doris Day and Rock Hudson, a barking cat that flew high overhead, a reindeer named Rudolph, and his little brother, sleeping soundly in a box.

THE CAPE

THE CAPE

PAUL LEFT AT 4:00 P.M., just as he'd intended, and, as he pulled from the parking garage, the weight lifting off felt, ever so briefly, like freedom. He'd been planning this respite for weeks, but had told no one, including Pam. Friends since high school, she alone knew his pain, and, to some degree, shared it. But what she felt wasn't the same, exactly, and no amount of "sharing" could make it so.

All week in the city, he'd been feeling the pull. There was something about Boston that usually made him feel lit from within; a spirit that kindled, giving fortitude. But in the past months, ever since Sean's death, Boston had begun to feel as if it were one enormous party, to which he had not been invited.

He'd first noted the sensation back in September. The weather had begun its procedural chill, prompting people indoors, and he began to notice all of the happy and laughing faces around him, in bars, shops, and restaurants, and realized that he wasn't among them. He could see them and hear them, clearly, but couldn't quite connect with their all-too-visible *joie de vivre*. It was as if he was a curator, viewing an artful display of smiles through a carefully polished pane of glass. And he knew he had a problem.

Paul had always been the first to a party. Not because he wanted to help the host, or was worried about punctuality, but because, as he had been since a kid, Paul was the type of person who didn't want to miss a thing. He'd been the child sitting up all night at the window, breathing and drawing on the glass, eyes peeled for Santa. He'd been the boy setting up a fireworks exhibition on the dining room table, with a precise list of the order in which they were to be lit. He so wanted to be *in* the moment, connected. What he was feeling now, however, felt anything but.

Here it was, just a few days before Christmas, and he was leaving happy, laughing Boston for the bitter chill of windswept Provincetown. Driving south, down Pilgrims Highway, Paul felt very much the pilgrim himself, voyaging into uncharted waters. He didn't know what he hoped to achieve with this visit, but everything about the journey to the Cape felt so right, he was certain reward would follow.

Paul had thought the deaths were over. He'd lost so many, back in the day, and lulled himself into believing that people—*all* people—were living with HIV; that it had become manageable. Until Sean.

Like other friends, Sean had been healthy, disease in check, which led to quite a shock, in April, when they met. They were at a coffee house, just off Boston Common. The entire park had begun to emerge, shedding its winter cloak to revel in spring. Flowers were budding, the air more temperate, and everything and everyone seemed on the cusp of change, fueling giddiness. But Sean, well—Sean looked as if his fire had been virtually extinguished. Shriveled and gaunt, it took effort for Sean to even smile, and Paul instantly knew that death, once again, had come knocking.

Death had taken virtually everyone Paul had cared about. Parents, in a car crash, many years past. Friends, lost to AIDS, cancer, drowning… And, perhaps understandably, this person who longed so much to *connect*, found himself—instead— detaching. He didn't want to care this much; to miss this much. The loss upon loss had taken its toll, shading everything in his world. Little things he'd enjoyed, like sipping from a hot cup of coffee on a cool morning, lost their pleasures. He was getting through each day, true, but at what cost? What effect does so much sorrow have on one's soul?

Passing signs for towns such as Sagamore, Sandwich,

Barnstable, and Yarmouth, Paul wondered why so much effort was expended creating inventive names for towns, and yet names for people usually came in the most conventional of packages. Mike, Joe, Katy, Sean, Paul...

Within those towns, how much was truly unique? What subtleties did they offer? They each shared commonalities, a store, post office, firehouse, stop signs, but what made them different? With people, however, even with the most simple of names, Paul could easily identify their uniqueness.

With Mike, it was his hair, always sticking up in the front, just so. And his laugh, like a lawnmower. Joe had the gentlest of manners, and his sweet smile... It could light up Paul's heart. Katy could be difficult, exasperating even, but her passion for social justice, her desire to help those less fortunate, softened her edges immensely, making her almost beatific. Sean, well, there was so much that was special, so much that made him *Sean*, he was impossible to sum up in just a few words.

And Paul...? Who was he? What made him tick? Paul had always thought that he understood himself, but he suddenly had found himself grappling with a very basic fact: he'd lost touch with his soul and had no idea how to get it back. That pursuit, in a way, was what had led him to the Cape.

In summer, the drive out could be endless, bumper to bumper, but in the dead of winter, Paul flew, and before he knew it, he had veered onto Commercial Street, nearing his cottage.

There was something about Cape Cod, specifically Provincetown, which soothed him. He found being so far out on the point, surrounded by dark ocean, comforting, if a bit unsettling, particularly as his cottage often perched over the water. *Swallow me*, he'd call out to the sea, late at night. *Cover me.*

Even though it was barely evening, tonight's sky was dark as midnight, with clouds obscuring the fragile quarter moon. The weight of the air told him rain would soon come, and Paul welcomed it. This had been what he'd wanted. Solitude. Quiet. Time to think, and process, and *feel*.

Putting his key into the lock, Paul knew this had been the right choice. A crazy decision, perhaps, but the *right* one, nonetheless.

It had been months since the last vacationer, and even with the quick burst of cold brought by the open door, the air within still felt still. Once inside, Paul began the rituals of opening the cottage, lighting a fire, unpacking, cleaning and tidying, until the cottage began to feel like home. Well, not *home*, exactly, but there was something about the blank slate of a vacation rental, missing the photos of friends and family and personal touches, which felt appropriate for his mood. He wanted to reflect, and not just on moments captured and memorialized in photographs. He wanted to comb through the tangled wires of his mind, and the muted anonymity of the space suited Paul just fine.

He'd bought the place years ago, and while at the time the price had seemed high, the improvements he'd made since meant that Paul could now sell it for five times the amount. Not that he ever would. The cottage was now a part of him. While he couldn't visit it as often as he'd like, just knowing others were enjoying it, keeping its spirit alive, provided a bit of comfort.

Running back out to the car, Paul hauled in his last items, a few bags of groceries. He'd brought enough provisions for the night, as he'd known Angel Foods would be closed. Soup would be enough, he figured, to take off the chill, together with a glass of Merlot, and he was right. Plugging in his cell, Paul saw that Pam had called, twice. He sent a text, friendly but firm, stating that he'd be back for New Year's Eve, but not before. And that, above all else, he didn't want constant reminders from the outside world. He knew she cared, but he also needed the space.

Done, he pressed the power button, resolving not to resume communications until his process had been completed—whatever that entailed and wherever it led him.

The dream came again that night, as it often had in the months since Sean's passing, and he was soon enshrouded in fog. In the thick gray, Paul found himself in a rowboat, at sea, with no oars. Realizing his plight, alone in the middle of the ocean, he found himself becoming fearful.

"Hello?" Paul cried out. "Hello? Is anybody there?"

His words echoed endlessly. He spun about, rocking the boat, but immediately steadied himself.

"Please! Can anyone hear me?"

There came no reply. Paul searched about desperately for any signs of life.

"I need help!" he called. "Anyone?"

Terror started to grip his throat. "Hello!" he cried. "Someone? Anybody? I need someone! I need help!"

But no one answered, and the waves continued their gentle lapping, long into the night.

The rain he'd been expecting came the next day, but he wandered through town despite it. While some shops were closed for the season, more were open than he'd expected, though he noted few shoppers. Those with whom he crossed paths nodded politely, yet with a slight air of mistrust. They were locals, clearly, and protective of their town. They saw themselves as guardians, though of what, exactly, Paul wasn't quite sure.

He meandered through shops, though he had no reason to do so. There were no gifts to buy this year, aside from Pam, and he'd bought hers mid-summer on Newbury Street, back in Boston. A shop near the Met Cafe had a display of amazing dresses, but what caught Paul's eye were the sheer scarves atop each mannequin, which seemed like fragile works of art. Though in all of their years of friendship he'd never seen her wear one, Paul had felt certain that a scarf would be just the right gift and bought one on the spot.

Pam was one of those people who was difficult to describe, because she almost didn't seem real. She was tough, but fair. Blue collar, yet could dress up, if need be. And understanding as hell, particularly for someone who worked in a mortuary.

She'd had the job when they'd first met, and seemed, to Paul's surprise, quite happy. In fact, Pam was virtually the only person he'd ever met who had no complaints, about anything. It wasn't as if her life had been easy, but somehow Pam had found a way to embrace every hurdle that came her way, viewing each as a gift. *An opportunity for growth,* she'd say. It was an attitude that Paul himself strove for, but could never quite capture. Life, he had decided long ago, was entirely unfair. To Pam, however, life just *was*. It was the looking for explanation, or the expectation of enlightenment, which caused unhappiness, she believed. But try as he might, despite her admirable convictions, Paul kept trying to understand. Why had his parents died, been taken from him, so young? Why had many of his friends suffered the same fate? The idea that someone (God?) was responsible and needed to be held accountable was a concept hard to shake. Paul needed someone to blame, and—looking around—only saw himself.

The sun never came out from behind the clouds, but Paul knew it was close to dinner time. He decided to splurge, opting for a table at The Mews by the window, overlooking the sea. The nearby bar glimmered, its hanging glasses reflecting the blue neon light above. Picking up the menu, he perused his options. Reminding himself of his pledge to eat vegetarian as often as possible, he selected the roasted vegetable and polenta lasagna, though it was the cod that caught his eye. Still, it had been a good and tasty choice, as was the glass of Zinfandel.

Music played remotely and diners chattered, but Paul was suddenly and acutely aware of being alone. He couldn't shake the feeling that he'd been thrust out on display, as if others were watching. With each forkful, questions would pop into his head. Was he shoveling too much into his mouth? Was his hair messed up or his zipper down? Did any of the other diners find him attractive? Were they feeling sorry for him, eating in this pricey restaurant alone? *Well*, he thought, *maybe people feeling sorry for me isn't such a bad thing. Who knows? A bit of human kindness, a little pity party, may be just the thing to help.*

He decided, right then and there, to shed his solitary shackles and *engage*. Happy with this decision, as he sat there, Paul began to smile. Grinning, he took another bite, as if a camera were just a few feet away, filming the lasagna's journey from plate to mouth. To Paul, appearing approachable meant looking friendly, and so he continued to smile, glancing about for someone with whom he could connect, until he came to the realization that the smile on his face likely looked more crazy-odd than anything else. Dropping the smile, he decided, instead, that it was up to him to take the first step toward *engagement*.

And so, as the waitress brought him his second and final glass of wine, Paul actually looked up from his plate, into her hazel eyes, which—until that moment—he hadn't noticed. "Nice night, huh?"

Her brow furrowed, skeptically, as she raised her eyes from his, glancing out the window. "If you like rain, it is."

Paul turned to view the sky, which was darker than ever, but when he turned back to respond, she'd already gone. *So much for engagement.*

Paying the bill, he rose, pulling his jacket tightly, zipping it all the way up. Stepping from the restaurant, the wind outside hit him like a smack in the face. It was brutal, unforgiving, and he knew it would be best to return home to the cottage.

But he wasn't ready for solitude. As much as he'd wanted it, initially, he couldn't handle that. Not yet, anyway.

With the goal of connection in mind, he turned, walking briskly past the East End galleries and through the center of town, until he eventually saw the lane that held the A-House. While a gay bar hadn't been in his plans, Paul instinctively knew that he needed to be around people, to be with his tribe, even though he'd never seen himself as a joiner.

Stepping inside, Paul loved how the red lighting and lit fireplace immediately warmed both body and soul. Having just finished half a bottle of wine by himself, he instead ordered a mineral water. Glancing about, he recognized a few local faces, but no one he knew by name. Not that he'd expected to. Still, there was a part of him that desired a connection. Not a hookup—that wasn't what this was about. But this idea of engagement hung over him. Paul wanted conversation, a meeting of minds.

Folks grouped about the fireplace, loosely, while a few other singles hovered around the edges of the room. They eyed him, curiously, as one would an amusing toy, with slight, distant smiles. This wasn't what Paul had envisioned. Looking about, searching for *connection*, Paul was about to leave when a cute guy approached, his hair falling into his eyes, and offered his hand.

"I'm Ben," he grinned.

"Paul," Paul offered, though he knew where this was headed.

"You live in town?"

"I have a place here," Paul smiled, "but I live in Boston. I just came out for—well, I needed a break from the city."

Ben nodded, combing his hair back from his face with his fingers. "Yeah, I get you! I live in New York, you know? So, it's like, ten times worse than Boston."

Paul nodded politely, not wanting to bash the city he loved, or city living, for that matter. There was a part of him that needed the Cape, which needed P-town, but he also knew that, wherever he traveled, he'd be a Boston boy at heart.

"So, *Ben*—what brings you to Provincetown?" Paul queried. He was attempting a nice, polite tone, to indicate he wanted only a conversation, not a blow job.

"Aww—-a wedding," Ben sniffed. "Can you imagine? A wedding? In P-town? Just a few days before Christmas? *Please!* What the hell were they thinking?"

"It's nice that you came—you know, to support them."

"Well, it's my brother," Ben stated, "so I didn't have much choice. This is where he and Julie met, so they thought it'd be romantic and shit to come back for the wedding." Ben launched into falsetto, *"Imagine! A winter white wedding, in a quaint little hotel, next to the fireplace!"*

Paul laughed, even though Ben wasn't being very funny. "Sounds like you don't like her."

"She's alright, I guess," Ben admitted, grudgingly, his hair falling again into his eyes. "Not the brightest, but sweet."

Grinning, Paul realized he was thinking the same thing about Ben.

"So are you here with friends?" Ben asked. "Family?"

"No…" Paul wasn't sure how to respond. How much did he want a stranger, even one so cute, knowing about him? He'd wanted a connection, but that didn't necessarily mean a soul-baring moment in the middle of a bar. "Well, I wanted some time to myself, so figured I'd get some quiet here in P-town."

"That's for sure," Ben laughed. "Half the places are closed.

And look at this dump…"

Paul took note of his cherished bar, which was already beginning to thin out.

"Dead."

There was something about the way Ben said the word *dead* which made Paul almost feel like crying. Instead, he attempted a smile.

"It is pretty slow tonight."

As Ben studied Paul, he again swept his hand through his hair.

"You, uh, wanna get out of here?" he offered.

Paul sighed, "It is getting late. And I've got a long walk…"

"No, I mean—with me?"

Even though he'd known the moment would come, Paul still felt flattered that someone, anyone, wanted him. He smiled. "You're really sweet, Ben, and impossibly attractive—"

"But—?"

"I really just want to go home. I—"

"Want to be alone," Ben finished, for him. "I get it. That's cool. Ever come to New York?"

"Yeah," Paul nodded. "Sometimes."

Reaching into his wallet, Ben pulled out a card. "Call me. When you don't want to be alone."

"Definitely," Paul grinned, then laughed. "This is one of those moments that I know I'll regret. Probably as soon as I get home, I'll be wishing you were with me."

Ben smiled, somewhat sadly, before pulling Paul to him in a hug. "Thanks. For the chat and—well—just, thanks."

Back at the cottage, Paul found that his words had surprisingly come true; he did miss Ben. While he recognized Ben wasn't the most ideal husband material, he alone had offered Paul what he'd needed most that night: simple human interaction. And that gesture imbued their encounter with far more meaning than warranted.

Flipping on his phone, he saw that—despite his prior message—Pam had indeed called back. He stared at the phone until his sense of obligation took hold. Putting the phone on speaker, he poured himself a final glass of wine.

"Hey hon, it's me," Pam's voice chirped, coming through loud and clear, as always. Paul could tell she'd been drinking, as that tended to trigger her more affectionate side. "Listen, I know you said not to call, so I'll make this short. You are my friend—my best friend—and I'm concerned about you. This isn't like you, to just run off. But I know you have a lot on your mind, so I'll obey. But if you're not back by New Year's Eve, fair warning: I am running all the way out to the Cape and dragging your sorry ass back. So be here, okay?" she paused, as if expecting him to respond. "Be here," Pam repeated, more gently. "Love you."

He stared at the phone, its lit screen brightly illuminated. *Pam loves me,* he thought. *One person, at least, loves me.*

The waves were at play that night, all night, like caffeinated children engaging in tug-of-war. They slapped at the deck, sometimes furiously, but something about the irregular thud, solid and sound, felt comfortingly like a heartbeat. While the house had heated quickly, the cool of the sheets made Paul burrow beneath, almost entirely. *"Cover me,"* he sighed to himself.

Finally warm, he stretched out, his left arm filling the empty spot beside him, and thought again of Ben. He didn't love Ben. Hell, he didn't *know* Ben. Ben was just a man—a young man— who had wanted him. But Paul realized that being wanted wasn't enough. Not anymore. He wanted someone to know him. To devour him. And not just because of his pretty face. He needed someone who appreciated him for who he was and what he had been through. Paul wanted someone, above all else, who understood.

Sean had been like that, though they'd never been lovers. They'd had a kinship, since that first summer, meeting at Herring Cove. Both by themselves, they'd settled near each other, unaware, only to find themselves sharing a laugh when an old, saggy man had skipped by, wearing a tiara and nothing else. Catching each other's eye, they exchanged jokes, then stories, finally moving closer and closer, chatting the day away.

Between the irritating greenheads, nipping at their ankles, the endless eye candy, and the amazingly picture-perfect day, they'd had a nonstop supply of conversation and found themselves hanging out not just that day, but the entire week, and every moment they could in Boston, until Sean's death.

Their friendship, that bond, couldn't be duplicated, but Paul knew he had to try. He wouldn't find another Sean, that much was clear, but there were other good, decent people out there. At least, Paul assumed that to be true. The more difficult task would be finding them.

It was crazy, Paul knew, given the frigid wind and gloomy skies, but the next day he nonetheless found himself biking toward Herring Cove. He'd awoken and discovered that Sean still occupied his thoughts. With others who'd died, Paul had managed to compartmentalize, to make peace, but Sean was different. Last night, thinking of him, Paul felt as if a giant cloak, a cape, had settled over him. And while the cape wasn't especially heavy, he realized that he'd felt that same feeling, the same pressure, every time his thoughts strayed to Sean. The problem was, even when Sean wasn't front and center, that ache never went completely away. It hovered, wrapping over him, ever-so-slightly, invisibly weighing him down.

Finally reaching the empty row of racks, Paul leaned his bike against the rail, not bothering to lock it. With a grunt, he turned, jogging down the path toward the marsh, until the soft sand made running impossible. Following the well-worn course, erased clean of summer footprints, Paul wondered why he was doing this; why had he biked all this way, in the dead of winter, to a deserted beach? It wasn't as if he hoped to see Sean's ghost. He wasn't hoping for kismet, or sudden revelation, or divine intervention. Then it hit him: maybe he actually was. Maybe Paul wanted Pam to be wrong, and to have that grandiose hallelujah moment of awakening, of shedding the cloak, and finding himself once again fully *Paul*. But how realistic was that?

Climbing the dunes, Paul paused at the top, surveying the beach, only to find it barren.

Empty, he thought, *just like me*.

But Paul wasn't empty, of which he was fully aware. If anything, Paul had too much. Too many thoughts. Too many emotions. Too many feelings, coursing through his veins, and no way to let them out.

Pam had always encouraged him to talk, but it hadn't felt right, somehow, talking with her. While Pam had known Sean, her friendship with him wasn't as intense, as immediate, as Paul's had been. She hadn't grieved as he had. They'd experienced a similar loss, but the effects, for each, had been dramatically different.

Sinking down with a sigh onto the sand, Paul promptly stood back up, wiping the water and grit from his ass. He'd forgotten last night's storm, but now had a wet, sandy reminder of it on his jeans.

"Fuck!" he screamed, loud and long. Another "fuck!" erupted from within, filling the air, if only for a moment.

The second "fuck" seemed to tax him, taking away his breath, and he bent over, hands on hips, with a sigh.

After a minute, he rose back up, and realized, with a start, that he was crying. Tears etched his cheeks and, once started, it seemed they would not stop. He let them come, for a change. *What the hell?* he thought. *No one can see me.* And he stood there, crying, as the clouds above continued to gather, until the droplets of sadness had finally run their course.

He stood, for a moment, looking out over the cove.

Was that it? he wondered. *Was that my cathartic moment?* He checked himself over, but found himself much the same. The cape was still there, he could tell.

Must I shed it?

In many ways, the cloak felt comforting. It was a reminder, if nothing else, of all he'd experienced. Whenever he mentioned *AIDS* in public, he could feel others retract. But for Paul, ignoring something so significant felt like betrayal. *What does it say about us*, he wondered, *that we can't even mention a disease that took millions of lives?* Still, Paul had to admit that he found the cloak also restricted him, ever-so-slightly, and there was something about it, its heaviness on his chest and at his throat, that sometimes felt as if it were trying to slowly suffocate him.

Later that night, showered and warm, Paul glanced again to his phone. Pam had not called, honoring her promise, and for that he was grateful. Still, it was nice to have someone out there, concerned about his well-being.

He thought again of the scarf he'd bought her and with a shock realized that the next day was Christmas. For someone so keen to be in the moment and not miss a thing, he'd come close to missing the biggest holiday of the year.

He hadn't decorated, which had felt right when he'd arrived, but Paul now found himself almost desperate for a tree, and lights, and presents. It was too late to buy anything; all the stores had closed long ago. Looking about the cottage, he searched, pulling open drawers and closets, for anything remotely seasonal. Finding nothing, he almost gave up, but then inspiration struck; he grabbed some paper and a pack of crayons left behind by a summer visitor. Ripping open the box, he began drawing: stars, ornaments, Santa faces, and even one lame-ass reindeer, which looked more like a dog than anything. He taped these pictures all around the cottage, covering doors, walls, windows and refrigerator with simple, organic tokens of festivity.

Finally at peace, Paul snuggled in, content in knowing that, in some small way, he was in concert with the larger world around him.

That night, the dream returned.

Paul awoke, alone in a rowboat, adrift on the sea with no oars. Thick fog surrounded him, preventing sight, but Paul somehow knew that, this time, he was not alone. He felt something out there, though he knew not what. His eyes searched about, uncertain whether the presence was a kind one.

Finally, he found the courage to call out, "Hello?"

His words rang out, somewhat tentatively, hanging in the thick air. "Who's there?"

Silence.

"I know someone is there. I can feel you. *Who is there?*"

The fog seemed even thicker than before. Paul squinted, determined.

"I'm here!" he yelled. "I know you're there, too. Who are

you? Why don't you say something?"

Paul felt his throat closing up, his nervousness growing.

"I know I'm not alone—I feel you! Who are you? Are you a friend? Foe? Big, scary monster? God?" The words tumbled forth. "Who the fuck is there?"

Finally, through the fog, he heard a voice, quiet and meek, and barely perceptible.

"It's me... Michael."

"Michael? *Michael Bowers?*" Paul questioned, "But—"

"And Peter," another voice called.

"Peter. Peter Singer," Paul repeated, as other voices called out.

"Tommy—"

Paul completed it. "Tommy Hagen."

The names continued, one after the other, more and more quickly.

"Carlos."

"Abe."

"David."

With each name, Paul felt as if a brick were being laid, inside his chest. Name by name, brick by brick, Paul felt himself growing stronger. He wasn't shedding his cloak after all, but balancing it with inner strength. He tried to remember a face for each name that was said, but so many filled the air that his chest finally felt full, and the voices stopped.

After a moment of waiting for more, but finding only fog, Paul tried to take inventory. He'd heard so many voices, so many long forgotten names; had one of them been Sean's? He couldn't know for certain, but there was something about the way his chest felt that told him that Sean, indeed, was one of the bricks within.

Paul turned, looking around him as the dense fog shifted, becoming clearer. The water was perfectly still.

Paul stood alone in his oar-less boat, only to realize that surrounding him were thousands upon thousands of boats, bumping next to his, each with oars. Only the people were missing.

The men were all gone, but had left Paul their oars. There

was a way out, he knew, if only he would grab hold, but the journey home was one he would have to go alone.

GIFTS NOT
YET GIVEN

GIFTS NOT YET GIVEN

THE FIRST FEW YEARS WERE EASY. Connie would buy something, usually pink and impossibly cute. It was hard to go wrong, after all, given Clarissa's young age. Clothes accentuated a child's beauty and were always praised, even if undeserving, as "cute!" But it became increasingly difficult, with each passing year, to figure out an appropriate gift for her daughter. Weeks, or even months, prior to each holiday or special occasion, Connie would find herself wondering, *What would Clarissa like?*

Her husband, Earl, was never any help. "This is your deal, Con, not mine." As if they'd had other kids with whom he did help. But Clarissa had been their only child, and would always be special, if only for that.

Connie could be counted on to eventually find something fitting, but the amount of time spent on the thinking and planning and strategizing was all-consuming: *Pink, I would imagine. But now that she's sixteen, is pink still in? Maybe something more modern? Hip? Should it be long or short? Everyday or dressy?* The choices were endless, encroaching on overwhelming. She'd check with Donna—she always knew what was current. Connie didn't want to embarrass Clarissa; after all, there was nothing more awkward than excitedly opening a well-considered gift, only to find yourself mortified by your parents' selection.

Thinking back to her youth, Connie found it amazing she even still spoke with her own mother, Lil. They'd had so many rows, over the years, and still did, many of which revolved around Clarissa. Back then, it had been *"You're too young," "The time isn't right," "Earl will leave you,"* or *"He won't want to marry you, once he knows."* Those arguments had long ago faded, eventually becoming what they fought about today: *"Clarissa is a teenager; she needs to do things on her own terms," "You really think you know best?"* and *"Why rock the boat, Connie? Let Clarissa make the next move."* In Lil's eyes, Connie would always be a stupid girl of 16, needing her mother's guidance.

Connie pushed such thoughts aside, refocusing on the gift. Maybe this year, for a change, it wouldn't be clothes. But if not clothes, what then? It wasn't like Connie could afford an iPod, or Nintendo, or whatever kids loved these days. She was faced with a limited budget and even more limited ideas. But that didn't stop her from thinking about it, unceasingly, morning to night.

Was putting so much effort into a young girl's sweet sixteen even worth it? After all, Connie had been Clarissa's age when she'd given birth. And she'd tell anyone who would listen just how hard that birth had been. The hours. The pain. As if she'd been ripped into two. It had been agonizing. And yet...

Turning sixteen wasn't half as tough as turning 30. That was truly agonizing. And Connie had found herself giving that marker just as much attention as she had about Clarissa, and what to get her, and what to make for dinner. She'd obsessed for months, turning "30" into a hurdle, something to get over. Yet, despite all of her worrying and fretting, building up to the big day, once it had passed, she realized she'd overreacted to the whole thing. But that didn't mean she wouldn't do exactly the same again.

Connie couldn't stop thinking, and that was part of her problem. She couldn't shut her mind off, even at night, and it sometimes felt as if her brain would keep whirring about, tossing thoughts and ideas around like a blender, in increasing speed, until everything would finally break, exploding into the atmosphere with a gigantic splat.

Her pills helped, but even they couldn't quite stop the thoughts. Even at her most relaxed, an image would seep in, and immediately her mind would gallop into gear, processing and considering and over-thinking matters long since settled. For even while things were peaceful, Connie was never truly at peace.

Clarissa, she thought, *my beautiful sweet girl. Imagine, turning sixteen. Learning to drive. Dating boys. Or girls, if that is what she wants...* It didn't matter to Connie. The particulars didn't matter. What mattered most was that Clarissa was happy—whatever happiness looked like to her and whoever that led her to be. Connie wanted Clarissa to be happy.

June 23, 2013

God, mom will not shut up. All she wants to talk about is my party, and what we'll do, and who will come, and what gift I want. I get so sick of her I want to SCREAM! And dad isn't much help. He wants to keep peace, that's all. He never takes sides, even if he knows I'm right. Jeez. Grow a pair, why don't you?

Julie says all parents are like that, but I'm not so sure. I mean, are they all crazy? Maybe it's a requirement, that you be insane to have kids. I know I don't want them... Well. I think I don't. But if I was with someone who did want them—well, we'll see.

I thought about having a skating party, but mom wants something more formal. I tried to tell her to just let me do what I want, but she acts like it's a big deal, when it's not. It's just a birthday. Whoop-de-doo. Yes, I get to drive, but dad's let me drive on the side streets all year, even though mom would kill him if she knew. He wants me to be prepared, and I am. But it's like mom's afraid I'll mess up my life. Shit, I can't even plan a party on my own. She doesn't trust me to do the right thing, even though this is supposed to be <u>all about me!!!</u>

Robbie wants to celebrate—take me someplace special—alone—but I know mom won't go for it. She's fine with him coming over when she's there, or doing things with friends, but apparently the minute I'm alone with him, she thinks I'm going to rip off my clothes and go to town. Obviously, she doesn't know me very well, although she thinks she does. I mean, maybe someday, but I'm in no hurry. And I'm not sure it would be Robbie. He's cute and funny/sweet, and I know he'd do it in a heartbeat, but there's something about him that says "Gas Station Attendant For Life," and I know that is <u>not</u> what I want.

I think I'm meant for better than this, and him—but I don't mean that in a stuck-up way. I just think I'm meant to do great things, even if that means moving out. The truth is, there isn't much here I connect with. My parents are—well, <u>my parents</u>—and even my best friends feel like they're just placeholders. In class the other day Mrs. Bell was talking about personality types, and I think I'm one of the odd ones. There was one which is kind of an observer. Who watch and *feel* things, and I think that's me. And there were only like 1% of the population who share that type. But the worker bees? There are tons of them, and it seems like most of those are the ones I've chosen as my friends. They seem totally content to work at the D.Q., or Kroger's, or whatever, and drink and smoke and talk about all the great things they're gonna do "someday," but I know—and <u>they</u> know—that they'll never even leave the state. For as much as they may bitch, they don't have a clue as to where they're going. Just like mom, all talk—<u>lots</u> of talk—and no action.

But I'm not going to settle. I'm going to do something with my life—you'll see. I just have to figure out what. And get through this damn party first! ☺

Summer had flown, so filled with "relaxing" that Connie was simply exhausted. She preferred to stay busy, mapping out each day, arranging her thoughts and prioritizing, but summer had a way of sneaking up and slipping past, without leaving very much to show for it. She much preferred fall, with its cool nights and the scent of smoke in the air, signaling that the holidays were just a wee bit closer each day.   Just the thought of "Back to School" was enough to perk Connie up, and led to even more lists and organizing.

In fact, as much as she loved Christmas, Connie lived for autumn. The trees slowly turned, growing richer by the day, and then leaves slowly falling, baring both branches and soul. Maybe it was the colors that made her so reflective, or maybe it was the chilled air and lit fire, or the scent of apples baking, or the beginning of holiday shopping lists, or—who knows what—but Connie dove fully into autumn, allowing its activities to bathe over, fueling her through its days.

It was easier, now that Clarissa was back in school. During summer, Connie worried about how her unstructured days would be filled, and the return of school meant knowing that Clarissa was contained and safe. *I wonder what class she's in right now?* Connie pondered. It didn't matter, really, but that was the way Connie's mind worked.

Earl had suggested the day trip, and Connie had agreed, though she didn't really want to. Driving all day to see leaves changing, when she could see them right outside her window, would mean she'd have another unproductive day to show for herself. Earl, however, had been persistent.

"It would do you good to get out," he'd said, as if he knew

better than she what would cure her. Connie didn't feel ill or out-of-sorts, but she complied, if only to shut him up. He'd been a good husband, all along, if not the most exciting.

When Connie had first told him she was pregnant, she'd fully expected him to run. After all, they were so young, they'd both had other plans for their lives and the idea of a baby had, understandably, frightened them. She offered him an out, fully expecting him to take it, but instead he'd chosen to stay. That choice was one she appreciated. Loyalty meant a great deal to Connie. She expected it from those around her, and protected others fiercely in return. Any comments made about Earl, Connie took directly to heart. Whether he was the "right one" or not was beside the point. Earl had been there for her, from day one, and never left. Despite all, he'd never left.

They drove upstate, along the Hudson River, taking the scenic route instead of the interstate. It meant many more stops, and braking behind those driving slowly, but Earl was in his element. He was driving his beloved Mustang, windows down despite the cool, harvest tones flying past, and the beautiful Connie Norton, gazing out, by his side.

Despite their many years, Earl continued to marvel that the former Connie Norton was now, officially, Connie Simmond. It seemed impossible that Connie had become his wife, and while she may have gained a few gray hairs and a few more pounds in the passing years, Earl found her little changed from the young girl he'd come to love. Watching her, next to him, blond hair blowing in the breeze, lost in thought, like always, Earl felt the luckiest man alive. True, she drove him crazy, with her endless planning, but Earl figured that was better than a life lived in silence. Connie had opinions, and plans, resulting in a lot of chatter, but he'd take that over the polite and perfunctory relationship his parents had any day. Moving around each other, never engaging—that wasn't the life he wanted. And the day that Connie had told him about the pregnancy, while it'd scared the shit out of him, he also thought, *At last, Connie will marry me.*

Where they differed, mainly, was with Clarissa. Both had specific ideas on how to best move forward, which were diametrically opposed. Connie longed for the immediate, whereas Earl knew you couldn't force a teenager, that Clarissa would come along in good time. It was pointless to try to change the situation. But Connie could not be convinced, and strategized constantly on how to best bridge the gap.

They reached Fishkill, stopping for lunch on Main Street. Pulling into a parking space, Earl braked abruptly, sending a bag of apples tumbling out onto the floor.

"Jeez, Earl, I'd like to live—at least until lunchtime," Connie complained. Earl just grunted, reaching back to scoop them up.

Connie got out, stretching. It definitely was fall. Christmas would be here before you knew it, so best get started planning. While Earl peered under the seats for strays, Connie wandered, staring at some cute dresses in a nearby window. *Which would Clarissa like? Any of them?* It seemed impossible to even guess. Earl came from behind, escorting her away from the window, as if he'd known what she was thinking and put a stop to it.

Inside the café, the scent of garlic and basil was warm and soothing, making Connie feel instantly at home. Everything on the menu looked good, complicating her decision. "Ooo— potato soup with bacon bits!" she exclaimed. "And did you see the desserts? Three kinds of fruit crisps? Heaven…" Earl nodded, for they did sound good.

The waitress approached. "Can I get you two something to drink?"

Connie looked up, taking note of the server, and couldn't stop staring.

"Soda? Tea? We also have a full bar, so…" She smiled encouragingly, but Connie just stared.

Earl spoke up. "Coffee, black, would be great."

"You got it," she nodded, turning back to Connie. "And you?"

"What's your name?" Connie asked.

"Me? Oh—sorry! I'm Megan. I'll be serving you today."

"Oh. Megan…" Connie wasn't sure, but suddenly she felt like crying. "I—I'll have a Diet Coke."

Megan smiled. "Diet Coke and a coffee, black. Are you

ready to order, or—?"

Taking note of his wife's befuddlement, Earl spoke up. "We need a few minutes. Thanks, Megan."

"Sure!" she smiled, moving on to another table.

Earl reached across the table, palms up, offering his hands to Connie. She grasped them firmly, almost desperately. She felt the tears coming, but tried mightily to will them back.

"Did you see her?"

"Megan?" he nodded. "Yep."

"She—she could've been Clarissa."

"Con—"

"Same age. Same hair, skin tone."

"It wasn't her."

"But it could've been."

Earl slid out from his side of the booth, moving to hers. He pulled her close, placing a tender kiss on her cheek.

"It's okay, Connie."

She allowed herself to melt into him, her silent tears finally coming forth.

Across the restaurant, Megan watched, touched by the two strangers' exchange. *How nice,* she thought, *for them to care about each other so...*

October 18, 2013

This is so stupid! I can't believe how little mom trusts me! There's a big Halloween party coming up, and she said she won't let me go, because she caught me and Robbie together & says I'm grounded. We weren't even doing anything!!! We were just watching TV, and mom freaked out. In a way, it makes me want to have sex with him. I mean, she thinks we are already, so why not??? But, then again, I know he's not the one for me, no matter how fun he is to hang with...

I don't think she realizes sometimes just how much she

pushes me. She tries to keep me safe, which to her means I don't get to do anything. But that's not what life is about. You can still have fun and be safe. She wants so badly to have more of a "connection" with me, and can't see that the reason we don't connect is because she tries too hard. "How was your day, sweetie?" "What did you do?" "Where did you go?" "Who were you with?" "What did they say?"... the questions just keep coming, like an overflowing toilet. Sometimes, I just feel like leaving, chucking it all and running away. But that takes money, or a willingness to prostitute yourself, which ain't happening.

The thing mom doesn't get is that sometimes the only thing we kids need is someone to listen. Just sit there, quietly, and take us seriously. But she can't do that. She makes a big deal over everything. To her, every single thing MATTERS! Sheesh, that gets tiring.

In a way, I understand. She's trying to make up for the fact that she's not my real mother. She wants to make sure I see all she's done for me, in case I ever seek my birth mom out. She's trying to make sure that, no matter what my birth mom is like, even if she's picture perfect in every way, mom will still be my "one and only."

The thing she doesn't get is, I have no interest in my birth mom. Well, I have a basic curiosity, who she is, what she looks like, but not much more. Those "soul searching" questions of "Why did you give me up?" are not for me. Because I don't care _why_ you did it—I care that you _did_. Whoever she is, she didn't care enough about me to keep me. She didn't care about me enough to exchange photos and letters, like my mom had requested, keeping the adoption open. She didn't care that one day I'd have questions and want to know more. She shut the door and threw away the key. Like she thought I was damaged. She fucking didn't want to know anything about me, so I want to know NOTHING about her. Loser. What a fucking loser. To have a kid and give it up. She should've known better, which means she's not very bright.

I'm a pretty terrific person, once you get to know me. But she WON'T know me—ever. She made all the choices, and even if they seemed right to her, they all seem pretty shitty to me. So I don't want to know her. Fuck her. She got rid of me and slammed the door. You can never say "I'm sorry" for that.

Christmas was still three weeks away, but Connie, for once, already had Clarissa's gift picked out. It was a white iPhone cover, with pink and orange 60's-style daisies on it. It looked hip and fun, and it met the thirty dollar limit Earl had set long ago. She could buy Clarissa whatever she wanted, as long as she never exceeded the amount.

This gold foil paper is really pretty, she thought, covering the box and reaching for a piece of tape. *I bet Clarissa will like it.* A white satin ribbon seemed just the right touch, and Connie took a moment to make sure it was just so. Sitting back, Connie looked at her handiwork and smiled. Rising, she took the gift into the den and showed it to Earl.

"Isn't it pretty?" she asked, clearly proud.

Earl looked at the gift, then back to Connie. "It's beautiful, Con. Truly."

She smiled softly, then nodded, heading upstairs.

Walking into Clarissa's room, well, the room that *would* be

Clarissa's, should she ever reach out to them, Connie crossed to the closet. Reaching inside, her hand found the pull string, illuminating the shelves. The gifts were arranged chronologically.

The first one was from 1997. It had been just before Christmas, nearly five months since they'd placed Clarissa for adoption. Initially, Connie had been fine, *really* fine, but there was something about the holiday that brought regrets. *I'll never see her open presents,* Connie realized. *I'll never see her play. Or know what she likes, or hates, or loves. I'll never know if she's happy.*

Giving up a baby was easy. She knew she wasn't ready, and neither was Earl. Jeez, they were both so woefully unprepared. And with a baby, all she'd thought about was the crying and no sleep and messing the pants. She hadn't thought about the baby being a person. Someone with thoughts and feelings and dreams.

They'd been driven to Social Services by Lil, a few months before Connie delivered. It had been a beautiful spring morning, which seemed almost too bright and colorful, too alive. Walking into the building, with its blue-hued fluorescents, Connie could feel herself becoming robotic. She answered the questions, signed the paperwork, and even smiled. But she never really *felt* the moment. That would come later.

She was glad it had been Earl. He'd been there for her, and still was, each and every day. Connie knew she was a bit cuckoo, but couldn't help it. It was okay to feel this way, to know you'd made a mistake, but she was clear that, someday, she would make it up to Clarissa. Someday she would make it right.

Clarissa was now almost sixteen and a half. That *half* was very important. Because when she reached eighteen, she would become an adult. Free to search for her mother, with no parental signature necessary. And Connie felt certain Clarissa would seek her out.

Clearly, Clarissa would be curious and possibly angry. She'd want to know where she came from and why they gave her up. And Connie was convinced that once they met, they'd quickly become the best of friends. They'd talk about who they were, what they liked, all of their experiences, and how Connie had always held out hope. They'd talk about Lil, and her damning influence, which led to the records being sealed. They'd talk about love, and how desperately important it was to both give it and feel it being returned.

And when the time was right, and Connie felt that Clarissa was ready, she'd take her up the stairs, to *her* room, and reveal all her many gifts, not yet given.

Acknowledgements

MY HEART IS FULL, thankful for the many friends and professionals who have supported my evolution as a writer. My thanks go out to Sarah Tyler and John O'Leary for their feedback on early drafts of this collection, and especially Joan Werblin, for her thorough notes and analysis. I'm particularly grateful for the ongoing support of the terrific group of fellow authors and publishers I've met through Twitter, including Gregory G. Allen, Jeffrey Ballam, Brian Centrone, Ken Harrison, Alina Oswald, Carey Parrish, and Arthur Wooten. A special note of thanks to another Twitter tribe member, author David G. Hallman, who went above and beyond the call of duty in reviewing this collection; his notes improved the manuscript immensely. I'm indebted to Sara Valenti and Ryan Bills of Sara+Ryan Photography for their expertise in making me look good.

I was fortunate enough to meet the delightful Rebecca Johnson many years ago. I appreciate her dearly as a friend, as well as for her copy-writing skills and gracious generosity.

So much of who I am today can be traced directly back to Shane Michael Sawick, who died in 1995. His appreciation of the holidays helped kindle my own, and I thank him for letting me walk by his side, even if for a brief time.

During my years with Shane, I met a wonderful circle of friends, including the lovely Stephen Chappell, who gave me the recipe for Orange Cranberry Relish which is featured in the story

Glenbourne, IL. It's still one of my favorite holiday dishes and I make it every Thanksgiving and Christmas.

I'm blessed to have some key friendships which continue to feed me. Bob Napack and Karen Jaker Napack, David and Lisa Letourneau, and Mary Kay Holman-Romero and Deb Romero-Holman—you have my appreciation for your years of support, our nights filled with laughter, and the many wonderful memories we've made together.

To my parents, Fred and Dottie, my sister Laurel Provenzano and her family, thank you for our many holidays. I'm sure you'll see hints of those within these tales.

Finally, I would like to thank my family, Russ Noe, Mason Edwards-Stout, and Marcus Edwards-Stout. Living with a writer isn't easy, given the time and quiet needed. Thank you for understanding when Daddy needs to write, and know that even when I shush you, I do so with love. The three of you have made an everlasting impression upon my soul and bring unimaginable joy to my life. My days—and the holidays—would be meaningless without you in them.

And, Russ, your beautiful cover design kicks ass.

KERGAN EDWARDS-STOUT is an award-winning director, author and screenwriter, and was honored as one of the Human Rights Campaign's 2011 *Fathers of the Year*. *Gifts Not Yet Given* is his first collection of short stories. His debut novel, *Songs for the New Depression*, won the 2012 Next Generation Indie Book Award in the LGBT category, was shortlisted in the same category in the Independent Literary Awards, and placed on numerous *Best Books of the Year* lists. Shorter works have in such journals and magazines as *American Short Fiction* and *SexVibe*, and he contributes regularly to Huffington Post, Bilerico Project and LGBTQ Nation. Kergan lives in Orange, California, with his partner and their two sons. He is currently at work on a forthcoming memoir, *Never Turn Your Back on the Tide*, and blogs regularly at www.kerganedwards-stout.com.

BOOK CLUB QUESTIONS FOR
GIFTS NOT YET GIVEN

Gifts Not Yet Given is a work of literary fiction and a collection of short stories by Kergan Edwards-Stout. To help generate discussion, the following questions have been created to help guide your book club.

What specific themes did the stories emphasize?

How realistic were the characterizations? Can you relate to any of the characters' predicaments? Do you identify with any of the characters and, if so, how?

Many of the characters are searching for their place in the world, grappling with issues such as faith and individuality. What do you think about their struggles?

What stories stood out to you as memorable?

Each tale related to a holiday. What do holidays signify? What is their importance?

The author chose certain symbols and imagery to highlight key moments in the stories. Why images stood out as being symbolically significant?

In what ways do the events in the stories reveal evidence of the author's world view? What do you think he is trying to communicate to the reader?

Overall, would you recommend this book to other readers? To your close friends?

COMING SOON

NEVER TURN YOUR BACK ON THE TIDE

A Memoir by Kergan Edwards-Stout

"If truth be told, and it always should, I was taken in by the view, as so many others, both before and since. For me, it wasn't the sea which proved my downfall, but a pair of eyes. Eyes, specifically, made to drown in."

Imagine thinking you had the ideal life. The perfect partner, on whom you relied and trusted. An infant child, newly adopted. You'd given up your job, to take care of your child, to ensure that he had a terrific life.

Then one day, you wake up, and instead of the life you've been living, you spot an email, not intended for you, with this text, blinking at you from your computer screen: "Rich is so good with my son."

Suddenly, the life you've led is turned upside down. Everything thought true becomes suspect. And you learn, quite quickly, that you can never again trust the person sleeping beside you.

If Kergan Edwards-Stout's life was a *Lifetime* movie, surely he would be played by Valerie Bertinelli, and his husband played by Harry Hamlin or some other charming hunk. But life is far more subtle than that. And the truth even more disturbing—for that email discovery was only the beginning.

Like the wash of the waves, crashing onto the beach, you never know if the tumult will bring glittering riches, highlighted by the sun, or dark, murky residue of questionable origin.

SONGS
FOR THE
NEW DEPRESSION

A NOVEL
KERGAN EDWARDS-STOUT

C
circumspect press

Songs for the New Depression
Copyright © 2011 Kergan Edwards-Stout

C

circumspect press

Library of Congress Control Number: 2011915793
ISBN: 978-0-9839837-1-2 (hc)
ISBN: 978-0-9839837-0-5 (pbk)
ISBN: 978-0-9839837-2-9 (ebk)
10 9 8 7 6 5 4 3 2 1

Book Jacket Design by Russell Noe

Printed in the United States of America

PROLOGUE

JAMES BALDWIN ONCE WROTE that Americans lack a sense of doom, yet here I stand. Although I am not entirely certain that doom is indeed what brought me here, except most literally, that yin-yang, sturm und drang, heaven and hell push-pull has guided me, nay—ruled, since I saw my first hairy chest. Though others have struggled mightily in their quest for self-acceptance, for me, being gay has never been an issue. And in all of my hours spent contemplating the propriety of acting on such desire, I have encountered no downside. For if all roads lead to that same dreary destination of death, why not take the more enjoyably scenic?

Opposite, on the Right Bank, Sacré Coeur perches on the horizon, the late afternoon sun turning its pure white travertine a rich shade of gold. Without bitterness, I offer it a nod, acknowledging its divine providence in leading me to this place.

Wind, bracing here as always, whips through the crowd, prompting a herd of elderly tourists to warily step back from the edge. Watching, I wonder why they bother. For if, by some strange twist, one *had* been swept up by the prevailing thrusts of the invisible and flung to their death, would it truly have been tragic? Perhaps they would have had an hour, a day, or even twenty years more, but eventually they would have died just the same, albeit in far more perfunctory fashion. But to plunge from la Tour d'Eiffel? Can there even *be* a more spectacularly impressive departure?

This is a trip I have made many times, but never alone, and never to stay. Now that I am a denizen, my appreciation of Paris is bound to be different; in fact, ordained to be. How I pray, though, that the old pleasures will still taste as sweet. Please, let my former haunts retain their familiar allure! If there is any justice, permit my memories to register as before, unaltered by time or circumstance. For if I am here, and yet everything changed, how will I ever find peace?

The elevator doors send a rush of Japanese out onto the platform, forcing me back inside the vestibule. Turning to view the glassed tableau of a mannequined Monsieur Eiffel visiting with Thomas Edison, I consider my finger-smudged reflection. Not quite as forced as the figures before me, nor as dusty, but not altogether normal, either. My skin retains its ashen tint and the brown of my eyes is somewhat hazy. Still, given the road I have traveled, I could look worse.

It seems impossible that my choices have led me here, to this spot, drained of every ounce of life. Despite my long-held belief that one's journey—or ride, if you will—holds more importance than one's destination, I am no longer so cocksure. For if I, at age 17, had been handed a snapshot of myself as I am right here and now, providing the gift of foresight, isn't there a chance I might have chosen a different path?

Monsieur Eiffel gives no hint as to his view, appropriately leaving Thomas Edison to pop the requisite light bulb above my head. I linger, but none appears.

Perhaps I would have ended up here, regardless of choice. Perhaps it was destiny. Fate. An unlucky draw of the straw. Whichever, it is much too late to ponder, for no amount of wishing can change who I am or what I have done.

Were my life a play, it could easily be broken into three acts: before, after, and redemption. But while living, I never was able to step back, untangle myself, peel back the layers, and see things for what they were. Aside from Jon, life seemed confusing, filled with uncertainty. Now though, I can see that had I just made one single decision differently, all that came aft could have been forever altered.

While the tourists just beyond "ooh" and "ahh" at the surrounding sights, I stare into the masks of Eiffel and Edison, pondering the need for such a display. What could its creators have hoped to achieve? No matter how lifelike, these poses cannot possibly compete with the city below, teeming with the laughter and terror collectively known as "life."

I am about to journey on, shaking my head at their folly, when a thought occurs.

Perhaps these figures serve not to compete, but to remind. Remind us that, in spite of our vision of an omnipotent God, pulling our strings and jangling our nerves, it is the human who debates, chooses, and acts. It is the human who regrets. It is the human who remembers. And it was a human who envisioned a skyline commanded by a metal sculpture of grace, stature, and beauty—and built it.

But for that conscious decision, Monsieur Eiffel's vision would have remained purely spectral. He would have died, just the same, and none would have been the wiser. Wandering along the Seine, tearing chunks from our baguettes, we would have been blissfully unaware of the gigantic hole gaping high above our heads. But, happily, Monsieur Eiffel resolved to act, and this marker upon which I now stand, etched on so many souls, remains as proof of his ride.

PART I
GABE: 1995

"Shiver Me Timbers" by Tom Wait
Track 1A, Side B of Bette Midler's album,
Songs for the New Depression

GABE: 1995

WITH MORE THAN 200 holiday CD's alone, it is impossible to choose. The music must be subtle, bittersweet, emotional—but not weepy. Dance music and rock are out, so skip ABBA, the B-52's, and Blondie. Karen Akers, although I love her, is much too wobbly. Kathleen Battle and Sarah Brightman at their most ethereal could work. But nothing overtly classical. Whenever I hear that at some queen's funeral, I think, "Jeez, she never listened to that! Put on some Jerry Herman."

If I was doing this my way, as I truly wanted, all that would be played upon my demise would be Midler. As in Bette. The Divine Miss M, herself. But I don't need the backlash that would cause. Perhaps, if I'd died in the 80's, I could have pulled it off. But not now. No, little Miss M ruined everything when she cashed that first tainted check from Disney. She may have gained a billion more followers by selling out for celluloid stardom, but not fans who really understood her. What the masses got was an airbrushed Canter's waitress; a Celine Dion who tells fart jokes.

In any event, Miss M need not worry about saving a date for the festivities. Exactly when my demise will be, I can't really say, as not even I am desperate enough to commit suicide merely to guarantee a clear date on my friends' calendars.

The choice of music, though, is extremely important. You want people to feel comfortable enough to grieve, or laugh, or flirt, but not so comfortable that they have a really, really good time. ("We had *such* fun, we're coming back tomorrow!") Cunt-ree western is out, as is techno, rap, bluegrass, jazz (too disorienting), children's songs, and fado. About the only thing left is cabaret, which I simply will not put my guests through.

Anyway, it's too late now for any grand decisions. Jon went to sleep hours ago. Although how he can sleep at a time such as this is beyond me. Has he no compassion? No soul? That I should be up at this dark hour, unable to rest, and yet he slumbers peacefully... It's unfair, to say the least.

Well, perhaps I'm the one being unfair, overstating my case. To clarify, my T-cells are currently at "acceptable" levels, I haven't had any major infections since '93, and the drugs seem to be working. Currently, my viral load reads as undetectable, sending my doctors into giddily optimistic spasms. But I'm not convinced. I know that, somewhere, deep inside where it counts, this virus is gaining ground, gnawing through me quickly and voraciously. Despite the doctors' proclamations to the contrary, I know that I will not survive the year. It is not a lack of willpower or strength that will do me in, it is the virus itself. I've always known it would get me, and am at peace with that knowledge. In fact, there's something empowering in giving myself over to the disease. Now, *I* can control *it*, instead of the fear controlling me. Not that I can lessen its affect or stop the disease—or that I want to—but that I can ride this kayak down the river and over the falls, without being thrown out along the way.

"For Christ's sake," Jon cries out down the hallway. "Will you turn out the light and come to bed? You can die tomorrow."

My always-sympathetic husband. But he's right, in a way. Tomorrow, I just might die.

Upon reflection, I realize that your image of me right now might be a bit skewed. Actually, kind of fucked. I am neither a nihilist, inordinately depressed, nor jaded. Though I can be and have been all of the above, and fully expect to be again.

But I have been battling this monster since 1987 and have learned that, for me, going along for the ride is easier and less taxing than fighting. Giving myself over to HIV is actually an act of self-preservation.

And despite, or maybe because of, the advances in treatment, my body is now on the decline. The doctors can quote any outstanding test result they want, but one quick glance in the mirror tells me all I need to know. For example, I now have AZT butt, defined as a loss of muscle and visible sag. (My ass, once talked about all over town, now looks suspiciously like a Shar-Pei, prompting even more talk around town.) And my face... My face, alas, has changed, too. Inflamed lymph nodes have given me a jaw line resembling a boomerang. And the combustible combination of pills, gel caps, tablets, capsules, shots, powders, and Satan's sperm, which I devour daily, has ignited a flame that eats at my face still, leaving harsh lines and cavernous skin. The only noticeable physical improvement has been the unexpected emergence of cheekbones. Jon jokes that I'm just like Jodie Foster. But it is a hollow laugh I give in return, for I know that it is not age which bears such features, but death.

Awwwwwww! Jesus Christ—Morbidity 101. Again. Gotta change that fuckin' channel. Find me some happy talk.

Jon has been a godsend in so many ways. And yet, he's also the biggest pain I've ever met. To say that I was initially attracted to him would be a lie. Taken individually, Jon's physical assets are quite remarkable: full, eager lips, curving into a grin, small round glasses hiding dark, penetrative eyes, ears that tilt forward slightly, giving him the look of competent listener. But once put back together, Jon's looks can only be described as Geek-Meister. That I should love him so still takes me by surprise. For when we first met, I was neither searching for, nor desiring, a partner.

In 1993, having wandered for years through a world of darkened back rooms in sticky shoes, I found myself suddenly dumped into a brightly-lit fluorescent world of doctors' offices and hospital hallways. Unexpectedly, and with unnecessary irony, a fatal disease prompted me to save my life. With dramatic swiftness, I violently shattered the cockpit window and pulled my war-torn body from the self-induced wreckage.

Out of work and desperately in need of a job, I perused my resumé. With past jobs including substitute teacher, interior designer, sales (art gallery and retail), bathhouse attendant, actor, and jackhammer operator, my future was mapped out for me as clearly as the skies above: my destiny lay in AIDS education. I had all the qualifications necessary: I was cute, needed work, and possessed the ability to become histrionic over even the smallest non-issue. In short, I was the perfect candidate for the world of non-profit. (It is important to note that today I would not get that same job, unless I could also become histrionic in Spanish.)

And so it was that I arrived at the Los Angeles Department of Eat, Drink, and AIDS; otherwise known as LA-DE-DA. Given the above-mentioned qualifications, I was quickly promoted beyond my ability level to the position of Director of Volunteer Resources. As I'd never been a director before, much less a volunteer, I was somewhat nervous about the demands of the job and wondered if I had what it would take to succeed. I quickly learned, however, that my past jobs proved instrumental in my new role as Emperor of the HIV Kingdom. From my stint of substitute teaching, I'd learned how to separate unruly children, which proved invaluable in brokering peace between the warring Directors of Education and Communication. From my extensive experience of selling clothes at J. Jacobs, I had learned to guide volunteers to the programs in which they were needed, regardless of fit. And from my days picking up cum rags at Club Way-Ho, I had learned how to give expert blow jobs, which is essential for volunteer retention.

And it was in this glorious, heady time that I found myself leading our weekly Vogue (Volunteer Orientation Group), as one of my serfs had called in sick. Of course, we in the Vogue knew that the real reason Miss Thang called in was because she was down on her knees pleasuring a well-known local weatherman at his historic Los Feliz home.

But as Miss Thang was otherwise occupied, it was I who addressed our new recruits that cloudy Thursday evening. And it was I who took note of the geeky volunteer's cute cowlick.

And it is I who holds my dear, loving Jon in my arms tonight.

"Where is the research?"

"Do I look like Dr. Gottlieb?"

"So, what—you implicitly trust everything you're told? You swallow whatever your drug company-sponsored doctor tells you? That could be what's killing you!"

I took a deep breath before responding. In these new volunteer orientations, you usually get a bunch of sheep, but you never know. Sometimes people wander in off the street...

"Well, Mr. Frank—"

"Jon—"

"Jon." God, I liked them feisty. "Do I know for certain that HIV causes AIDS? No, I do not. Could it be that AZT actually causes AIDS? Probably not, but I don't know for sure. But I do know this: the odds are in my favor. You can believe in conspiracy theories, or think the doctors don't know what they're doing, or that AIDS is caused by eating blue cheese and pork rinds when the moon is full. Believe whatever you want. But within these walls—these hallowed walls of LA-DE-DA— our message is this: HIV attacks the T-cells, leading to a weakened immune system, which is susceptible to illness, which can lead to death. That is what we believe, and that is what we teach. Now." This guy had me so riled, I almost forgot there were others in the room. "Moving on..."

Jon's hand shot up into the air. "But if you're not certain—"

"Jon, I'm not certain I'll be alive to get up in the morning, but I brush my teeth at night just the same. I have a choice: do I believe all I've learned about HIV since working here, or not? And do I trust that my knowledge is correct? Do I trust that every pill I take will work its magic on me? I don't have to believe it, but I do. I believe it with every fiber of my being. I trust it, and all I'm doing, because I want to live."

In a perfect world, the volunteers would have remained silent for a moment, savoring my impassioned rhetorical skill, praising my brilliance while wiping racing tears from their cheeks. Then there was Jon.

"But—"

I exploded. "Goddamn it—what the fuck are you doing

here? Why did you walk in the fucking building? You could be at ACT UP. Or on a Tina Louise Hayride. Or at a Course in Gobbledygook... Why are you here?"

For a moment, it was silent. Jon focused on his feet before looking up at me with the most pained eyes imaginable. "I'm here because I'm scared. I'm scared—and I want to help."

Being challenged isn't necessarily a bad thing, so long as the aim is to better and strengthen rather than tear down. And better is exactly what Jon did with me, on a daily basis. Although assigned to the Phone Friends program, which met in the building's windowless dungeon, Jon stopped by each day, popping his head into my office to say hello. At first, he got on my nerves. But soon I began to look forward to his daily assaults. Stupid, challenging people are annoying, but with smart people, the sparring becomes an aphrodisiac.

We began to meet after work. First, it was only coffee. Oh, how The Abbey walls burned with the fire of our discourse! Seeing our eyes locked, faces flushed, as we debated everything from politics to plays to the existence of God, others would veer quickly away from our table, fearful of being singed by the flames. Coffee soon turned into dinner, dinner into movies, movies into concerts, concerts into everything. We became inseparable. And yet...

We hadn't even kissed. The fervor from our conversations was so intense that, by the time an evening had ended, I'd often feel as if we *had* had sex, so wet was I from perspiration. Perhaps we feared that the physical could not possibly surpass the emotional. But that didn't stop me from fantasizing.

I'd lay awake for hours, stroking myself lightly as I imagined his fingers brushing mine. The images were never salacious. I dreamt of his face, impassioned by rhetoric. His arms, tense with meaning. And that lopsided grin, warily admitting that I might have a point—one that he would thoughtfully consider.

Luckily for Jon, though his opinions were often misguided, he did not suffer from a lack of intelligence. He knew when he was wrong and was open to learning more. Emotional and psychological growth were stimulants, inspiring him to further his experiences and delve more deeply into the unknown.

I, on the other hand, was usually correct in my views. Spurring him on, I often felt as if I were his personal 'Enry 'Iggins, preparing him for the ball. I never voiced such thoughts, certain that he would disagree, but I did find pleasure in knowing that I wielded that power.

Being infinitely generous, I would gently prod him toward important books, music—anything that he might have overlooked in his studies. Plus, my varied life experiences aided immensely in Jon's search for self-discovery. Indeed, much can be learned about life by cleaning rooms littered with used condoms.

"You're so fucking irritating," Jon exploded, shaking the walls of my office. "No matter what the topic, you think you're right."

"Moi?"

"It's more important for you to be correct than fair."

"What's wrong with honesty? Just because I have a wide range of interests—"

"Can't we talk about things without taking sides? It's the struggle to expand oneself that's important. Not just choosing—or *guessing*—correctly."

I paused, letting his anger subside, as I knew it would. "What, exactly, are we arguing about?"

Jon reached into his backpack, pulling out the match that would ignite our first full-blown fight.

"This." In his hand he held a CD. The original cast recording of *Cabaret*.

"Where—?" I stammered. "How did you get that?"

"I had it at home." He handed it to me. "Read it."

"But—"

"Read the credits."

"Look," I said, trying to slip the CD onto the desk unnoticed. "Let's talk at lunch. There's a great Thai place—"

"Read it!" Jon shoved the CD back into my hands. "Out loud."

"Can't we just...?"

With a force I didn't know he had, Jon spun me about, marching me into the outer office. Cupping his hands, Jon beckoned my busy volunteers. "Come on, everyone! Gather round! Witness a sight unseen in 30-some very-odd years. Your tireless leader—for the first time ever—will publicly *eat crow!*"

As a crowd quickly gathered, I tried to make a break, but the encroaching swarm pushed me back to Jon's side.

A blonde bimbo intern, unfamiliar with our strange tribal ways, bopped into the office, "Hey, gang, what's going on?"

One volunteer answered, "I think they're raffling off a prize. Some kind of bird."

"No," said another, crusty nose ring swinging. "It's a lover's quarrel."

"Those two are *lovers?*" gasped the intern.

"Not yet," said Mucus. "But just watch."

The crowd assembled to witness my humiliation now surpassed that of our most recent fundraiser. Jon stepped onto a chair. "Ladies, gentlemen, and girls, thank you for being here today to witness the unbelievable, the unfathomable. A most incredible act will occur," he paused. "Gabriel will be proven wrong."

A gasp ripped through the assembled, for they knew that such a moment was not likely to be repeated in their lifetimes.

"That's right, my friends. Our own Gabe Travers will own up to a mistake, publicly and humbly."

The volunteers eyed each other worriedly. Even if I had been wrong in the past, I'd never admitted it. I am a firm believer in stating what you have to say with conviction, especially when uncertain of the truth. Would I, these volunteers' diligent leader, their moral compass, submit?

Jon stepped down, gently pushing me toward the chair. I made a whispered plea. "I'll give you anything... The keys to my kingdom!"

He pushed me from behind, more forcefully. "Read."

Shakily, I stepped onto the chair. The room was silent, breathless with anticipation.

I gave it one last desperate shot, yelling, "Quick! Janet Jackson is over in the food bank!"

The bleary-eyed queens eyed me savagely. I should have known better than to try that with a breed able to sniff out celebrities at 300 yards.

And so, in an unnatural voice, audible only to animals and gossip-loving queers, I began to read.

"Uh, *Cabaret*. The new musical starring Jill Haworth, Jack Gilford, Bert Convy, and Lotte Lenya." I coughed, clearing my quickly gathering phlegm. "Boy—look at that! Joel Grey gets billed below Bert Convy. What does *that* do to your self-esteem, huh? And speaking of Joel—did anyone else catch him on *Brooklyn Bridge*? Not bad, huh? Or how about in *Kafka*? Wow, is he an entertainer or what?!? But that daughter—Jennifer— whoever told her she was an ingénue? If only she'd stuck to character parts..." Sensing the lack of responsiveness, my patter slowed to a trickle.

"We're waiting," Jon persisted, arms crossed adamantly. I looked again at the credits.

"Book by Joe Masterhoff. Based on the play by John Van Druton and the stories of Christopher Isherwood." I stopped, unable to continue. "This is really hard for me."

One volunteer reached up, taking my hand in his, "It's okay, honey. We're here for you."

The bubble-headed intern turned on her heels. "I don't get this. You guys are way too faggoty for me." The nearest queen viciously shoved her to the door, kicking it closed behind.

"Continue," said Jon.

I hesitated. "I—. Uh, music... music by John Kander. Lyrics, Fred Ebb."

"Who?" queried Jon.

"Ebb. Fred Ebb. Music and lyrics by Kander and Ebb."

"Not Kurt Weill?" Jon pushed. "Not music and lyrics by Kurt Weill?"

"No," I admitted, the CD hanging limply in my hands. "Kander and Ebb. Kander and Ebb did *Cabaret*."

"Well, what did you think, honey?" gasped one nearby queen. "Everyone knows that!"

As the room burst into a swell of gleeful satisfaction, so happy to see me taken down a notch, Jon took my hand, pulling me down from the chair and into my office. Shutting the door, I could still hear the excited voices beyond, replaying my humiliation for latecomers.

"It had to be done," Jon stated, not as excuse, but as fact. Unable to respond, I sank silently into my chair.

For the next hour, Jon tried to talk with me. To get me to see the wisdom of what he had done. But it was futile. He had embarrassed me in front of my colleagues. He had orchestrated my public humiliation and expected gratitude. Rather he, Jon said, than someone who didn't care about me.

When, after getting no more from me than a shrug, he finally left, I pondered his definition of caring. Whereas our past tangos had been harmless, stimulating even, this felt like betrayal. Maybe I had it coming. In fact, I'm certain that I did. But that knowledge did not mitigate my pain.

For the next two weeks, I screened all calls, took my lunches early and out, and generally did everything possible to avoid contact with Jon. It was not only anger that kept me in flux, but the fear that, in planning my downfall, Jon knew more about me and my anxieties than anyone. And if he could know such demons and be unafraid, maybe he was someone I could truly love. But if his invasive act had, in fact, been a maliciously lucky strike, aiming entirely to wound, then—frankly—Jon Frank spelled trouble.

"You only hurt the ones you love." This astute assessment of the human condition arrived courtesy of my best friend, Clare. Friends since high school, Clare is the one person I can count on for empty wisdom drenched in meaning. Perhaps it is because her name is an anagram for *clear*, leading one to assume that her very being is focused and stable. Or that her similarity in name to *clairvoyant* imbues her with special powers. Regardless, somehow Clare is able to utter incredibly vacuous sayings which, upon passing her larynx, become instilled with such dignity and significance they can stand up to Gandhi.

"Wow. You know, Clare, I think you're right? We *do* only hurt the ones we love. Why didn't I see that before?"

Clare shrugs, shoveling another fork full of Chinese Chicken Salad ("Dressing on the side, please") into her already overflowing mouth. Although painfully, paper-cut thin, Clare was cursed by delusions of chunky cellulite, viewing herself as one big box of Velveeta. As such, she continually alternated between the latest fad diet and intimate encounters with Hostess snack products.

"You know, Jon may have hurt you, but maybe there's a reason for that. Maybe you can turn that pain into a positive."

"Yes, that's it!" I nodded enthusiastically before becoming lost in her continuing platitudes.

As she talked, I studied her, taking in every movement. Her jaw muscles, tensing and straining as if they were the legs of a quarter horse trying desperately to reach the finish line, never did. Instead, her jaw flapped on and on, veins pulsing, as her invisible horse raced endlessly onward, furiously circling the track, as if on some unaired episode of *The Twilight Zone*. And it seems that I am the jockey, screaming in terror the faster she runs, the stadium swirling maddeningly as I search for some means of halting the sickening ride.

The image blurs as my thoughts somehow land on Clare at age 16, hiding her slender arms beneath a frayed fisherman's sweater, two sizes too large. She had reached out to me, become my friend. One of the few. And yet I wondered why.

Was she so enjoyable that I couldn't bear to be away from her? Sadly, no. Did her emotional nurturing offer me solace, sufficient to endure her less-endearing traits? Hardly. I viewed Clare as a handball wall. I could bounce things off her, knowing that she would return the lob, however inefficiently, somewhere in my general direction. But the things I needed now, such as depth and nuance, were beyond her grasp.

Why do I keep such people as Clare in my life, I wondered, when I get so little from them? True, she has always been there for me... But is loyalty enough?

As I observed her mouth, continuing its gallop, my eyes began to glaze like the limp piece of ham on the plate in front of me, before veering over to the nearby waiter's perfectly rounded ass. God, why are there so many cute waiters in the world?

Why can't they be accountants? Stockbrokers? To waste such beauty on food service...

"So what does Jon say about this?"

With Clare finally back on planet earth, I returned as well. "I don't know."

"What? You mean you haven't talked to him?"

"What is there to say?" I stared at my barely picked-over meal. "I didn't do anything wrong. I mean, I *was* wrong. Factually. But motivationally? No. My motive, my drive, was simple human discourse. A talk about musicals. Every queen's fallback discussion. That I would confuse my composers is excusable."

"This, from the very person who picketed Dan Quayle?" God, Clare could be annoyingly accurate. I decided to ignore her.

"But to throw it in my face! To make a mockery in front of everyone." I lapsed into silence, pained by the memory.

Clare, just for a moment, put down her fork. "You know, dear, that you are my favorite person with a penis in the entire world. You are funny, sporadically caring, and smart. Perhaps too smart. That you are wrong, even occasionally, isn't the end of the world. But just look at what the past few weeks have done to you. You're a mess! Give up the ghost, honey. It's not worth it."

"If my dignity, my sense of self, isn't worth the fuss, what is?"

Clare eyed me steadily before picking up her fork. "Your health?"

I paused, looking again to the beautiful waiter, gracefully pouring water from a pitcher. Clare was right. To have HIV is one thing. Almost any gay man can deal with that these days. But to be a diseased, down-trodden, worn-out victim of AIDS, spending my days wrapped in a fringed shawl... Better to be like a waiter after all, who, despite the fire in the kitchen, greets each customer with a carefree and welcoming smile.

Upon returning home that evening, I entered from the garage, as usual. I wouldn't have discovered the enormous package if Maxie hadn't slumped against the front door, emitting little yips. I didn't even have to look at the card to know it was from Jon. Setting it on the coffee table, I stared intently at the cardboard box, wondering what on earth could be inside, before quickly ripping it open. In it were close to 20 CD's and albums: every Kander and Ebb recording ever made. *70 Girls 70, The Happy Time, Chicago, The Rink, Flora the Red Menace,* and more. Everything in existence, from A *(The Act)* to Z *(Zorba.)* I was astounded.

Then I noticed another package, wrapped separately, at the bottom of the larger box. Opening it, I broke into a huge grin. *Cabaret.* And not just the original cast recording we'd fought over. There were also CD's of the film soundtrack starring Liza (never better), the 1966 London version (with Judi Dench as Sally Bowles—wouldn't you have loved to have seen *that*?), a symphonic version by the Royal Philharmonic, vocal highlight albums, and original cast versions from Italy, Austria, Greece, Hungary, and Israel.

Unable to stop myself, I began to cry. For someone to care that much, despite all, was more than I'd ever dreamed possible. Pushing aside the jewel cases (a truer name there never was), I picked up the card:

Just as you have taught me, so I shall teach you.
Musical Theatre 101. Class begins tonight at eight.
My place. – J.

The ringing of the phone broke my revelry.

"Yes, yes, yes! I'll be there!" I shouted joyously, almost tonguing the receiver.

"You'll be where? Did we have plans?" my mother asked, confused as always. "Are you coming here or something? I didn't make dinner. But we could go out..."

In my life, I long ago learned that my mother alone had the ability to destroy even the teensiest bit of happiness by simply saying "hello." She never calls or drops by at an opportune moment. It's almost as if she is being cued by some unseen stage manager, timing her entrance for maximum devastation.

And so it was that, instead of responding to her garbled thoughts, I hung up the phone. I knew that there would be hell to pay later, but I simply could not—would not—let her ruin my moment of bliss. Instead, I celebrated the package's arrival with a shower and douche, then called Jon.

So cautiously did he answer that I knew he was as uncertain of the next move as I. I thought seriously of punishing him by giving sullen, uninspired responses, but instead rushed giddily into an overblown declaration of my affection and desire. My words tumbled forth unguarded, so grateful was I to finally release my thoughts, until I finished, and was met by a moment of stunned silence.

It was only later, at his apartment, that words were replaced by actions. Although nervous, I happily let the moment carry me into sexual oblivion, where loving kisses and forceful gropes gave voice to our promised coupling.

Screeching, endless and unvarying, rang in my ear for a full fifteen minutes before I finally jumped in.

"Mom, I'm sorry! I had a problem with my phone—"

"For a week? You're telling me your phone was down that long?"

"It's fixed now."

"And during that time, your voicemail miraculously survived, recording each message? Including mine? And still, you didn't call? You're telling me that for the entire week you haven't made one single call. Not even from work."

"It wasn't intentional," I lied. "I just, you know, forgot."

"Forgot your own mother. That's a fine how-do-you-do."

"Can't we drop it? I'm calling now."

"You know I spent eighteen hours in active labor. Eighteen."

(Now seems to be a good time to note that I often feel that those who believe that homosexuality is caused by genetics are barking up the wrong tree. Though many may protest, every gay man I have ever met has a mother who is, in some manner, domineering. That they would have passive husbands who retreat to the den to escape their wives is understandable. In fact, it is a tribute to the gay man's sensitivity that, despite our mothers' ability to harangue, we still love them so. It is in this vein that I relent.)

"Of course, Mom. You're right. I'm sorry. I should have called. Can I take you to dinner tonight to make it up?" (I've also found that domineering mothers love free food.)

"Oh, so now my son who does not care enough to pick up the phone actually wants to pick up the tab?"

"Yes. Definitely. Your choice."

Without hesitating, she jumped in. "Café La Boheme. Cocktails first, at the bar, then dinner. Maybe dessert afterward at Sweet Lady Jane's, if they're open. Make the reservation. Pick me up at 7." Click.

Moms. Gotta love them.

Arriving at her house, I am stunned by what greets me. Given, it has been two months since my last visit, but never the less I am at a loss. My mother has shed approximately 30 pounds, had her hair cut and lightened, wears a fashionable red jacket with oriental detailing, and seems to have had a facial peel. For some reason, she just glows. Forget for a moment that this sixty-some suburban housewife is my mother—she looks hot!

Trying to brush aside such thoughts, I stammer.

"You look—Wow! Amazing."

"I do, don't I?" This is said neither rudely, nor without a small measure of pride. Though she has always been attractive, recent years have seen her as if through a haze. Never quite of the times, yet not entirely out either. Although my father died many years ago, it is as if only now has Gloria emerged from her cloud of depression.

"So—what?" I ask pointedly.

"What what?"

I look at her closely, trying to find any trace of the woman who raised me. "How do you explain this? Are you dating someone? On the hunt?"

"Would you believe I've found God?" she asks, double-checking for her house key before pulling the door closed.

"Where was he hiding?"

"You think I'm joking? Open the car door for your mother.

No wonder you don't date."

"I do date, for your information. But tell me more about God. Have I met him?"

"Is it so hard to believe that I've found solace in the word of our Lord, Jesus Christ?" She holds my stare, daring me.

"Oh fuck. Mom, I have enough worries in my life without you going off the deep end."

"Far from it," she says, as we pull up to the valet. "I feel better than I have in years. I've let go of old issues... Resentments. And I'm happy. Truly happy. What could possibly be wrong with that?"

Honestly, I have no reply. I wish I could be as happy as she sounds right now. As the valet opens her door, she steps out.

"Thank you." She leans back to me with a wink. "Now... How about some martinis?"

As she sashayed up the restaurant steps, I took some comfort in the notion that, even if my mother had indeed found herself a new house of worship, she was still driving there on the same old fumes.

SONGS FOR THE NEW DEPRESSION
IS AVAILABLE NOW IN HARDCOVER, PAPERBACK,
AND ALL E-BOOK FORMATS

CPSIA information can be obtained at www.ICGtesting.com
Printed in the USA
LVOW13s0210300813

350255LV00002B/12/P

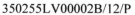

9 780983 983736